IT HURTS

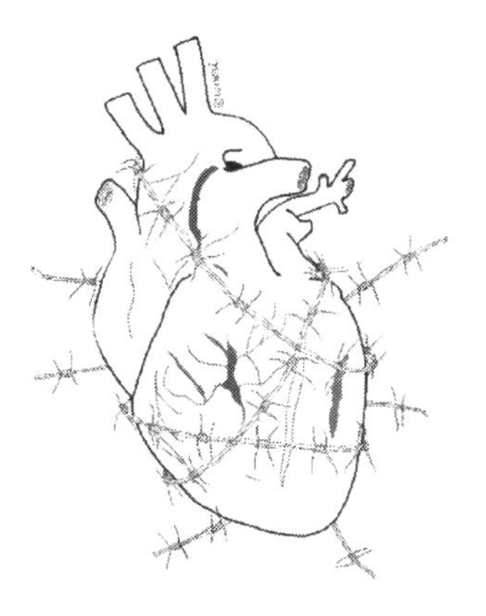

Magesoul Publishing

A TRILOGY OF ANTHOLOGIES: BOOK 1

IT HURTS

Publisher:
Magesoul Publishing
PO Box 580019
BRONX, NY 10458
www.magesoul.com
@magesoulpublishing

Editor: Natalie White

Book Cover & Illustration Design: Adric Ceneri

Interior Format and Design: Adric Ceneri & Natalie White

ISBN: 978-1-7342908-5-1 (Print Version)

IT HURTS

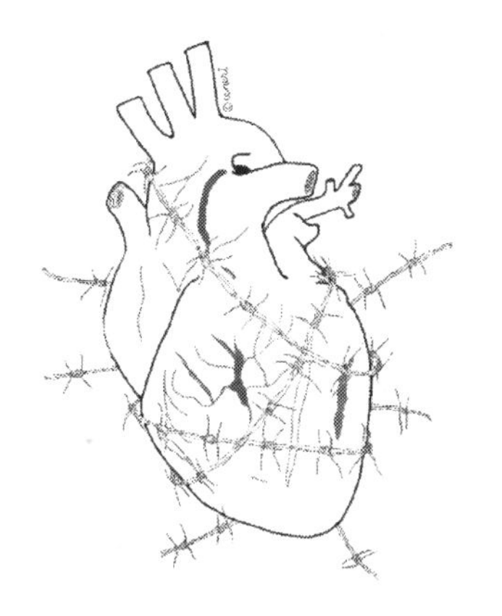

THIS BOOK IS DEDICATED TO...YOU

Define Pain.

Acute. Chronic.
Psychological. Physical. Emotional.

Its depth cannot be compared nor quantified, as no matter the origin, pain can only be measured by our own individual experiences and our own interpretations of such experiences.

As humans, when pain makes a home in our souls, we are not always able to articulate just how much, *it hurts*, but as artists we are blessed with the ability to transform such pain into art.

"It Hurts" is an anthology created by 15 authors, who have bled themselves into their own personalized chapters, expressing in their own words what it means to hurt, in a unique collection that shares their traumas, hardships and loss, with one aim in mind…

To remind you,
you're not alone.

TRIGGER WARNING

This publication asked each author to provide content that was related to trauma, pain, loss or suffering and as a result contains an extensive variety of written content, a proportion of which, may be considered violent, graphic or distressing to some readers. As such, discretion is advised.

If you are triggered and require support, you are strongly encouraged to seek help from your personal support network or reach out any one of the agencies listed below:

NATIONAL SUICIDE PREVENTION LIFELINE (USA) - 1800-273-8255

INTERNATIONAL ASSOCIATION FOR SUICIDE PREVENTION:

https://www.iasp.info/resources/Crisis_Centres/

• • •

CONTENTS

Dedication --- 005

Shattered Foundation - KM Quinn --- 009

The Breaking - Natalie White --- 031

Untitled [Like my Life] - Jorge Anton --- 059

Lived [Devil Spelled Backwards] - Cedrik O. Wallace--- 083

The Aftermath - Kristin L Provenzano --- 101

Embracing My Fears - Adric Ceneri --- 117

Emotionless - Erica Varela --- 139

Even Angels Fall - Angela Marie Niemiec --- 151

Broken Pieces of Togetherness - Alex Le Gare --- 171

L.O.V.E.-Four Letters That Hurt - Unknown the Poet--- 191

My Soul Didn t Break, It Saved Me - Soshinie Singh --- 205

Love Can Never Hurt - Parth --- 219

Finding My Voice - Brooke Story --- 235

CONTENTS [Continued]

247 --- Memories - Carlos Medina

259 --- A Day in The Life - Jacob Marley

290 --- Books by Magesoul Publishing

292 --- Coming Soon

293 --- Other Books by the Authors

Shattered Foundation

KM QUINN

ABOUT THE AUTHOR

KM Quinn is a Mexican-American poet, writer, and soon to be author. She was born in Mexico and raised in Texas. Having traveled the world and living overseas during her 20's, she has settled in New Jersey with her husband and two kids after separating from the US Navy. She has been writing since elementary school because reading was always an escape for her and writing became a way of rewriting stories to make them hers one word at a time. Some of her other interests include sketching, painting, and a true love for aviation. Her writing concentrates on the topic of love, but life and lust make love a messy subject to write about, all of which you can see spill into her work. A Home Author and part of the Editorial Team for Magesoul Publishing - be on the lookout for her upcoming debut book, "In Between The Lines", coming soon in 2020.

Connect with her on social media:

 @wax_poetically

:::

Shuffling through
a pile of keys,
panic sets in and coldness fills me.
I haven't been here in so long,
I forgot what the key to this locked
door looks like anymore.

My hands continue to tremble,
it still feels familiar
but forgotten.
Slowly, the echoes of every click
matching the rusted old piece of iron
ring in my ears.

I hold my breath,
I haven't faced you in so long,
your screams, still in my head.
Terror sets in
and I try my hardest
not to make a single noise.

I haven't changed much,
since the days when you engraved in my head
that the silence of someone, as unwanted as me, is best
A rush of bad memories come to me
like a roaring sea, with waves ready
to submerge everything in their path

You were never a storm to be reckoned
with and yet you had such a destructive
beauty to you, no one could look away.

It almost made you look deserving
of that three-letter word,
foreign upon my trembling tongue,
each time I'd visit and say—

"MOM".

⁝⁝⁝

I remember the days when it all began.

The prescription pads
and all the pens lying around
in the glove compartment.
The horrible mood swings and
sudden forgetfulness.

How, you had conversations with
invisible people only you, could see.
The only thing that would calm you,
were our weekly drives to the local pharmacies
which I considered "spending time together".

I knew it was wrong, even though
I was very young at the time,
but I didn't care because you
looked so happy and
that made you smile more, than I ever did.

But it was always
the end of the week
that was frightening,
your horrible tantrums and the
yelling that pierced our ears.

Even as I look back now,
I'm not sure I would have stopped you
from faking those signatures
because I liked seeing you happy,
and those colorful pills
always brought peace,
to your aching soul.

:::

You tried,
I know you did.
I could see it in your eyes,
I could feel it in your estranged hugs
and occasional kind words.

All the school events you attended,
dressed in your best to impress,
with a smile so bright,
no one would've ever believed
the internal struggle
that was happening within you.

You were always the best
with the crowds,
and you believed every lie
that slipped through your lips,
but I knew you better.

I was the lucky one
you showed your true self to.
Sometimes I wish you had realized,
I was not mentally capable
of handling that at such a young age.

But you treated me as your best friend
because you knew,
I would never tell.

I prayed and I prayed that one day,
you would just wake up better,
because I knew you tried your best
not to listen to the voices in your head
or let the rain make you sad.

Against all odds
you always lost the battle
when they got too loud for you,
and screaming at us,
masked the muffled sounds
inside your head.

I know you tried your best,
even if your best
left us feeling
so unworthy
of life.

:::

I wish you had taught me more
about life and how to love.

I wish you had taught me life
isn't always bad
and love doesn't always
break your heart.

I don't know how I am supposed
to trust someone will love me
and not disappear, when you,
always said *"I love you"*,
right before every disappearance.

How can I believe life can be good,
when you made it so hard for us?
Even in the good times,
you found a way to make us,
feel the sorrow.

I've been going through life,
guessing and taking my chances,
like I know what I'm doing.

I've had my fair share of failures
that fell nothing short of being
devastating disasters.

I wish you would have taught
me more, but how could I possibly
expect this from you,
when no one ever taught you more,
or better?

How could I expect you to love me?
When no one, ever loved, you?

:::

It saddens me to think of what
a normal day for you is like.
Sitting there all alone in a
room full of pictures.

The cross you bear, gets heavier, as the days go by.
There isn't much you can change now.
The regret is heard in your voice when we speak
but sometimes I wonder, if you even know why.

I wonder, if you even realize
your children grew up without a mother,
even though you were standing,
in the very same room as us.

You still battle your mind on the days
when you feel the loneliest.
I hope one day you get the chance
to feel relief from all that weighs heavy in your heart
and tortures your soul inside.

I hope one day you find a way
to forgive yourself for it all.
I hope one day you're able to let go
that of which has caused you the pain
you unleashed on us.

I hope one day I can love you
the right way and then maybe
you'll know what it feels like to be loved,
for the very first time.

I hope one day you will know,
I forgive you…

I just can't forget.

:::

A hundred things
I could have learned from you
but all I learned was that love,
is meant to be painful...

That love, like a rose,
is worth holding on to,
even when your hands are bleeding
from the thorns digging into your skin.

You, let love shatter you,
until you had felt every
crushing ounce of pain,
you could take, and that is why,
you always tried a little bit harder,
and stayed a little bit longer,
because, you loved her.

Despite the torment being induced
on the lives, you two created, you stayed,
allowing us to absorb her pain,
like sponges, soaked in water.

You stayed, so you wouldn't have to
care for us alone,
but it did not help us.

You should have left her long before
we became punching bags in the corner,
as therapy for her mad mind.

You should have protected us better,
Instead, you made us believe love,
was agonizing and that was somehow ok,
because at least you weren't, *alone.*

:::

I waited and waited.

It felt like forever as the days went by,
watching the sun rise and the moon light
my lonely nights—

I waited and waited.

For you to call my name, to reach for me too.
How could you leave me behind?
When I needed you, to guide me?

I waited and waited.

Sometimes I ask, why I wasn't worth your time?
Why you didn't turn back?
Why would you leave, just me, behind?

How could you leave,
your only daughter to fend for herself,
in a world full of monsters,
with no defense?

I grew stronger of heart and stronger of soul,
stronger from everything you failed to show.

But I waited and waited.

And instead of turning back
to grab my hand,
I was forced to see you
turn your back to leave.

Forced to watch as you faded,
further and further away from me.
Left full of questions,
I'll never be given the answers to.

Still I stay…*Waiting and waiting.*

While you pretend not to remember the day

...you left me behind.

:::

It only takes one person,
to make you feel lonely.
It only takes one person,
to make you feel nothing.
But I was lucky because I
had two people to make me
feel all this and much more.
The ones I longed for,
in times of trouble,
The ones I needed,
when the world was dark.
I reached out many times
but it always seemed to be
my fault, that my arms weren't
long enough to reach out to you.
And sometimes I wonder if maybe,
you kept moving further from my grasp,
just so I couldn't grab your hand.
It only takes one hand to help you out
of the pits of hell, yet neither of your
hands were available, always too busy.
All I wanted was one hand to pull
me up and out of that treacherous
world I was living in.
While you remained the *hands*
that were always
out of reach.

:::

I finally saw the reason behind
the steps you chose to take,
far, far, far away from me.
It wasn't me at all, that you feared,
it was the fact that you saw her in
my eyes every time I was around.
A mirror image of the woman you
once loved, that tore you apart.
You feared you'd grow to hate
me just like you did her,
so, you packed up your bags
and you left out the door
not a single thought of the heartbreak
you were causing in me,
All the pain I felt still lingers inside.
I lost my heart that day the door
closed behind you.
And I've grown to wonder
if I'd ever trust another man
to love me and keep me safe,
When the one who helped give me life
couldn't love me enough to show me,
I was worth staying for.

:::

Chains continue to echo in my head,
they were never really there
but I could always feel them,
weighing me down.
I still feel you pulling at them, every day.

I am always on the edge,
uncomfortable in my own skin
and now your voices,
speak to me too.
I try not to listen to them
but they have become so loud,
I can't shut them out,
and the more we talk,
the louder they get—

The sound of your voice
makes my night terrors want
to come out and play,
leaving me with sleepless nights.
You keep calling and calling
and I am left unable to breathe.

If only you could see
the fear that fills my eyes
with every single one of your calls.

My pain has become your new addiction
and I simply cannot continue
to be the medicine,
that calms your storm.

I am no longer, your child to control.

I struggle to find a way
to keep you alive in my thoughts,
when you've brought so much pain
to my life
and you continue to …

break

me

down

instead of …

up.

me

building

:::

I have a fear of everything now.
I'm trying to deal with the trauma,
I'm trying to let it all go,
but how can I forget,
when you,
have enslaved me for life—
You act like I owe you,
when I never asked for this life.
Everything hurts, from the inside out.
My bones are brittle and weak,
my mind is a mess
and my heart has remained broken.
I write everything down except
what's inside my head
because I've become afraid,
of my own thoughts.
I cannot close my eyes without
seeing you there.
The pressure keeps building and
you do not let up,
you keep pushing and pushing
for more, when you gave me so little.
You're expecting a payback,
but I am broke
from the emotions
that keep drowning my soul.

:::

The wounds have healed,
but the scars remain buried deep beneath
where no one can see them.
Inside, I still feel them,
when I am all alone
and I allow myself to visit the days
when we were all together—
It's not often that I go there,
I only visit once a year
much like the holidays,
it is exhausting
and draining,
This home I remember is
too much to handle
and I wonder how the child in me,
ever got through a day
stuck between these walls
covered in pain—
Hallways so dark,
even Jesus, would pray to himself.
As goosebumps rush throughout my body
I realize my strength was built brick by brick
and with no foundation
to hold these walls up, still,
I stand ***strong.***

The Breaking

NATALIE WHITE

ABOUT THE AUTHOR

"Sunshine, with a chance of thunderstorms."

Spilling ink is considered to be a therapeutic process fo
Nat, who is an Editor, Home Author and part of the
Executive Team for Magesoul Publishing. A deep
interest in books was evident in her childhood, but the
'need' to write evolved after two of her four childrer
were diagnosed with autism in 2016, changing her worlc
overnight, when she was required to give up her caree
and become a fulltime caregiver. In order to comba
isolation, this Aussie-born soul, reconnected with the
world through words, joining the Instagram writing
community in 2017. Creative by nature, she holds a
special interest in photography, music and graphic
design. This is one writer who doesn't consider what she
writes to be poetry, but rather a mosaic of thoughts, a
choreography of emotions, that somehow all blenc
together to express the language of her soul. Her debu
collection 'Salted Caramel Tears' is currently available
on Amazon worldwide and her second book 'Sage
Infused Rain' is scheduled to be released in 2020.

Connect with Nat on social media:

 @natwhite.au

:::

For as long as I can remember
I've had this unique capacity
to lose everyone I care about.
It's like some type of flaw that is visible
to everyone else, but me.
And I'm not sure how to change that
without changing everything,
I know myself to be...

I've spent a lifetime
biting my tongue.
So much so, that a faint line runs
on its underbelly,
as a reminder of all the times
I turned the other cheek and chose not,
to speak up.

I often wondered if I was doing myself
more harm than good.
Preferring silence over counter attacks,
while life's vultures seemed to hunt, in packs.
I faltered once or twice and realised
that all I did was add to the stench
of rotting flesh that lined my path.
Chose instead, to smile sweetly
at the hyenas as they laughed,
for they were not the first
nor would they be the last.

I told myself that just as every jungle has a King,
it also has a Queen, who has no need
to defend herself to the rest of the beasts.

Seeing myself as some,
"Florence Nightingale of Hearts"
(who'd made self-sacrifice, an art),
I carried baggage and solved problems
that were not mine to own.
I'd give until depleted,
and then, I'd give some more.

Created lines that could be crossed,
bars raised and dropped, on a whim.
Outside, completely fine —
a building avalanche, within.
Looked to others for approval,
when it was inside, that had to change.
The more I gave, the more,
unstable I became.

Arms wide open for the toxic.
Heart, a revolving door.
My desire to please, a disease,
and me, *its willing whore.*

A foreign concept the idea,
of a simple boundary.
I had no clue who was my friend,
and who, my enemy.

One by one the pennies dropped,
starting fires where they fell,
a helpless bystander surrounded,
by my self-fabricated hell.

Resentment brewed in my blood,
a slow-infused pot of tea.
A deep and brooding anger birthed,
the unravelling of me.

It was ugly, watching my own demise,
severing ties without remorse.
Unable to tell apart puppies, from wolves,
I annihilated them all.

It was messy, it was loud.
A head on heart collision,
the grinding sound of iron
crushing, aluminium.

And it hurt...

Like a cigarette stub pushed with intent
exposing nerves that screeched
in unwillingly flesh.
It was the closest thing to a sudden death
yet excruciatingly slow,
ending in a silence that delivered,
the loudest loneliness
I'd ever known.

As dawn broke in a field,
littered with the fallen,
I woke alone,
screaming,
"God, what have I done?"
Answered only by…
my echo.

And that's how I felt,
when it all fell apart.
When I, fell apart.
Like this perfectly functional, confident,
grounded individual
that I had spent my entire life creating
had just —
disappeared.

Every kindness, every good deed forgotten.
And there I lay, a pitiful mess,
stripped bare and exposed
for the pathetic creature I really was.

There was nowhere to hide anymore,
nowhere to turn.
Like the eyes of the world,
were all on me.

And the eyes of those who I loved
more than life itself,
looked at me in pity,
turning their backs, in disgust.

For across my naked body
written for them all to see,
was everything bad I had ever done.
Every fear I had ever felt
and every mistake I had ever made...

And that for me...
That, was what *'breaking'* felt like.

:::

It's back again.
I thought that maybe now
with my love, our love,
we could keep it at bay.

The taste of blood trickles down
from capillaries that have snapped
in the back of my throat,
from screaming your name.

I claw at the dirt with my bare hands,
desperate to reach you as fast as I can.
It's pouring with rain; the mud is thick.
Any progress collapses, the deeper I dig.

It's getting dark. I see you locked in the confines
of your mind-made coffin,
your darkest thoughts holding you captive
as the walls continue to close in.

But whilst the world goes on in technicolour,
seemingly unaware
of how much you are suffering,
I see you. I see you, like you once saw me.

And still with every stain and every scar
illuminated on your soul,
you're
everything I need.

The only thing that scares me,
is surviving without you by my side.
So I, turn my back on the light,
draw my sword ready and louder,
I scream your name again…

"Hold on love. Hold on.
And if you can't hold on to love,
hold on, to me."

:::

There was a time
I was worried it would be me.
Me, who would give him,
a million reasons to leave.
In the end his demons
were the one and only reason
he needed.
And I loathed them.
They didn't just keep him away
from me,
they kept me away,
from him.

"How much longer love,
must my arms be burdened
by the weight of your absence?"

:::

My fingernails
have been torn
from their roots,
holding on
to the edge of the cliff
you left me hanging on.
My arms are struggling
to hold my weight,
as I wait
for the inevitable freefall.
I knew what I was signing up for.
I can't say I wasn’t warned.
I knew you would try
to sabotage
what we shared.
Just as you knew,
like the masochist I am
…I’d stay.

⁝⁝⁝

My love
was supposed
to hush your monsters,
not wake them.
And now,
they are dancing
with my own.

:::

Tell me.
Look into my soul and tell me,
that all the things we talked about
and planned for,
were a figment of my imagination.

Tell me.
Tell me that those moments
where our eyes locked
and the rest of the world disappeared into oblivion,
were all, in my head.

Tell me.
Tell me that the single drop that fell
when you said you loved me
for the first time,
was merely "something in your eye".

Tell me it was all just a lie.

Tell me.
Tell me that somehow,
I orchestrated this whole thing
right from the start.
That the man I fell in love with,
was an imposter, a fake…
a mirage.

Tell me.

Tell me that every single time you swore
there was no way I could ever lose you,
that in truth, your promises,
were as empty on the exhale,
as the lungs that breathed life into them.

You want to leave? *Leave.*

But before you go, you owe me the truth.

Don't put your head in the sand and hide,
expressing you can't 'give me what I need'
as though it's me, that's caused you, to say goodbye.
Don't be so cliché as to tell me I 'deserve better'
at the same time as you turn away.

Hell yes, you and I both know I deserve better.
I deserve a conversation.
An explanation.

So, tell me.

Tell me it was all make believe.
Tell me and then maybe, just maybe.
I might have a chance at convincing
this beaten up, broken down heart of mine,
to let yours go.

But I know. You won't, you… can't.

Because it's not true.

And the fact that you
are all messed up and think
you don't deserve to be loved,
doesn't cut it because,
newsflash baby…

We are all screwed up.
Some, more than others.
We all have demons and goblins
hiding in our closets
and under our beds,
taking over
the space in our heads.

I saw yours were damn ugly...
but I chose you, anyway.

:::

I will never forget
the day or the month
or the feeling that came,
and never left.
It was a Friday,
in August.

And it stings.

Like my wrist was sliced
by the kiss of a lover
who promised forever,
and instead left me
bleeding out in a bathtub
of hollow vows
and shattered dreams.

::::

And until I see
your face once more…
time will tick,
(but cease to exist).
As I will exist,
(but cease to live).

:::

I am beginning to wonder,
if I subconsciously invite
souls into my life
that I know will let me down.
Feeding a festering wound,
reinforcing a childhood belief,
there is no soul in this world
who can love me,
in the way that I need.

Not even me.

:::

I didn't notice I was bleeding until now.
But there is something quite *poetic*
about the way my blood lingers
on the tiles below,
swirling around my feet
before making its exit down the drain,
taunting me, with its escape.

Unlike me,
trapped in a silent movie paused
mockingly on one frame,
searing into the back of my eyes like
an iron left a little too long
on white cotton sheets,
leaving stains that no amount
of bleach can treat.

A saline stream trickles down my face
in a slow and steady flow
almost instinctively in hope,
the salt will scrub me free,
of his filth.

But no matter how hard I try,
I cannot cleanse my mind.
And perhaps that, is the hardest part.
Of all the words ever used to describe me,
I never imagined they would be...
'Tattered and Torn'.

He might be gone,
but he remains a part of me now.
And I can't help but feel like it's
all my fault.

Curled up on the shower floor,
nursing my aching womb,
bile rising,
I gag at the thought of his touch,
It's all too much to process.
Too soon I let down my guard.
And for what?
To be held? To feel, 'loved'?
Too late my 'no's' came
in the form of whispers, falling on deaf ears,
my tongue panic-stricken, by fear.

But blame and shame now roar,
reminding me of the hefty price I paid,
for desperately wanting to numb the ache,
to fill the gaping cracks
you left within my grieving soul.

If you had stayed,
he never would have come
into my life.

Never would have laid a hand on
the woman you claimed
you wanted as your "wife".

And as I try to pull myself together
into something that resembles
some form of grace,
coming to terms that even though
I tried to say ‘no’,
my silence screamed ‘yes’,
I wonder…

"How will I ever be safe in the hands of another. . .
if I'm not even safe, in my own?"

:::

18 minutes.

In 18 minutes, I can get to the local shops and back. Pick up the kids from school. Make dinner. Write a poem. Hang up a load of laundry. Watch half an episode of my favourite TV show.

And 18 minutes is just how long they say it takes to die, or how long you have left to live, if you've been, *buried alive.*

18 minutes they say... so why, am I, still here?

("Breathe...)

Breathe? Maybe I'm the only one on the planet that feels this way but....

("Breathe...")

I'm hyperventilating at the mere hint of the 'b' let alone hearing you say it to me...

("Breathe...")

Breathe??

("Breathe...")

Breathe?!?

Can't you see?... I am!

And have you not thought for one moment that maybe, I don't want to. Maybe, I'm one of those people, who feels as though they don't have any other choice but to keep on living.

Maybe this version of life, needs an update, because mine didn't come with luxury options and I keep breathing whether I like it or not (in an involuntary, auto-pilot-function kind of way.... Like 'they' messed up in production, and I'm the version they need to re-call, because all I do is malfunction.). In other words…

Fuck. Everything. Up.

And yes - I just said that. In a vulgar, unladylike kind of way, because you know what? *I'm tired of living this way.* Tired of saying yes when I want to say no, of saying no when I want to say yes, reinforcing that it's ok for others to treat me in ways that are guaranteed to hurt me later. I'm tired of pretending to be someone different to who I am.

And maybe I don't even really know who I am. But I do know what I'm not. I'm nowhere near as happy and carefree as what I appear to be. For every positivity, there is something equally grotesque within me.

I'm not exactly sure how long I have been suffocating in these thoughts, but I know, it must be longer than one thousand and eighty seconds, that I've spent asphyxiating on the stale bread taste of self-depreciation. My soul now growling with hunger, begging on hands and knees, like a stray dog on the streets.

And maybe it's the fact that it feels as though a thousand knives are piercing my lungs each time I do take a breath or maybe the increase in CO2 is finally taking effect and screwing with my senses, but I spend days at a time romanticising about the smell of death's ugly stench and not because I want to leave.. no…but because…

I don't feel like I belong here.

I don't feel like I'm doing this right. Whatever this is. This life. Because I thought I belonged with you. To you. And woke up to find myself homeless.

And it wasn't the first time.

And if that wasn't bad enough, this time, all I had left was my dignity intact. And now he. The one who took advantage of your leaving. Took that too.
In less… *than 18 minutes.*

So, excuse me while
I hold my breath (in hope) …

My time.

Starts.

Now.

:::

It's been a while.
The words don't fall from my lips
like they once did.
They fall in dribs and drabs.
Here and there.
Like us.
Me here.
You there.
How. Did this happen?
I was so happy.
Flying.
Dreaming of you by my side,
for the rest of my life.
(Ha! Life. A knife. *Twisting in my spine.)*
There is no good in this "good"bye.
For hide do I,
a sickening truth behind this smile.
You know,
I would've waited forever
to lie in your arms.
Feel your hands on my skin.
You, from within...
but instead,
it was *him*.
Taking by force,
what I would have given to you *willingly.*
And still you don't know...

What happened to me.

Or how I was.
Or where I was.
Or what he...did.

One minute we were "we".
Then it was just, “me”.
And, “you”.
Almost as though,
I ceased to exist.
Forgotten in your ignorance.
No longer holding a place in your heart.
And maybe it's better that way.

Apart.

Believe me,
I'd rather you remember me
whole.

Besides.
I like the thought there is a place
I don't exist...
Because in that place,
the shame he stained
upon my soul
doesn't exist either.

"I have come to realise that you and I
are not as different as you may think, my dear.
while you live wishing for death,
I am dead wishing for life"

Untitled
[Like My Life]

JORGE ANTON

ABOUT THE AUTHOR

Jorge is a New Yorker, born & raised in Queens. Both a visual artist and writer, he's been writing since he was 14, when his then English teacher convinced him to join the Poetry Club as extra credit or fail her class. Though he enjoys reading, he's never read a poetry book and doesn't feel that he's been influenced by any specific poet, rather allowing his mood swings and life experiences to influence his writing, which arrives in all forms and subjects, from the innocent and romantic to the extremely dark and suicidal. Jorge feels life itself is poetic and therefore, why would you not find romanticism in expressing all of its forms? Having also always held a keen interest in photography, he tries to combine both art forms as best he can when either a photo he's taken inspires him to write or he writes a poetry piece and goes in search of a picture to capture a scene for it.

"They say a photo can tell you a thousand stories & it is true, they can, but sometimes they just need someone to tell it for them."

Connect with Jorge on social media:

@justmerlin [Words]
@iamjustmerlin [Images]

:::

Remember?

Remember the days when you'd take me to the park and watch me run around? I'd sit on the swing, waiting for you to push me with an endless smile on my face, one that would carry over as I saw my feet fly into the sky, where I'd reach for the cottony clouds, and test the sweetness of their candy. When those clouds ran tasteless on my lips, I'd jump off and make a quick dash to the set of slides across the playground.

From the swings to the slide was a rattling bridge on chains, which I ran across in jumps and skips to make them rattle loudly, and once I reached the center, I'd turn back to see you smiling at my silliness.

"Oh, silly boy, you'll wake the dead with all your silliness and laughter," you'd say over and over again not caring if I did as long as I was running around happily, like all little good boys should.

Remember when I finally made it to the top of the tower, where the slides waited for me to pick a side? "Should I take the straight slide down or the curly swirl that'll bounce me back up to the top? Wait, is that a fireman's pole?"

I had been down so many slides already so I slid down the pole instead, as you watched me with an approving smile on your face. Next, I'd run over to the monkey bars and climb them; remember I'd hang off them from my knees and make silly faces at you?

I remember those days clearly; I'd feel such joy in my heart when we headed to the park, you'd leave my Mom home with my baby brother and take me to the playground to watch me play.

Only, you didn't watch me, did you sir?

You never saw me run around searching for you or waiting on the swing to be pushed by you. I'd sit there looking up at the sky, wishing you'd show up, and give me a little push, until one day I did get a push, but not from you. You weren't there to stop the big boy from pushing me off the swing because he thought I was taking up his turn to reach for those sweets floating in the heavens.

Remember when he chased me across the rattling bridge, and pounced on me at the center of it, and beat me around, making the bridge rattle like crazy? You don't, do you? "Oh, silly little lonely boy, without a Mommy or Daddy to watch over you, I'll beat you 'til you're fucking dead, and don't you fucking cry to anyone or I'll fucking beat you again!"

When the beating finally ended, I'd make a quick dash to the tower, where I would hide my tears by painting them into the walls. Once calm, I always took the slide down, except for that one time I decided, if maybe, just maybe I came down the fireman's pole, I'd impress the big kids at the playground, and they'd leave me alone.

So, I took the pole down, but somehow lost my grip and so I took a straight drop to the bottom, hurting my ankles. Still, with my pain, I managed to get up and pretend none of this hurt.

Limping over to the monkey bars, I'd climb them, and sit at the top for hours, searching in every stranger's face the recognition of you, but you were nowhere in sight, ever. Then I'd hang upside down from the highest bar, to see the world upside down, and see if it were different then; see if you'd be there for me, there and then, but you never were, ever.

You'd take me from my mother's loving care and dropped me off at the park like it was a daycare center, where I'd be watched by a guardian of sorts, only there was none, was there? You'd tell me to stay within the playground's ironed out fence, otherwise, the boogie man would get me, but you never told me of his little demons prancing around the same confines you'd abandoned me in.

Then one day it all changed, it all changed for that one day, and you actually watched me. On that day, on our way to the park, we picked up two strangers, a woman, and her three-year-old child; you took us to the same park as always. You told me to go play with her child and show him the playground.

“Do you think they’ll get along?” she asked as she sat on your lap. “Of course, they will cariño. They’re the same age, why wouldn’t they?”

⁝⁝⁝

A Jester & Her King

I always wondered
why there were borders
surrounding her kingdom,
undiscoverable lands
I was not permitted
to cross into & explore,
but now I know why;
where I thought I was king,
she's shown me
I was simply a jester, her jester,
the one keeping
her entertained,
as her true king
remained dormant
in the shadows of her lies
until she was ready to send me
back to the dungeons
of her abandonment,
but I beat her to it
and left her on the
side of the road
to dwell with her
self-prescribed loneliness
alongside her true king,
right where she abandoned him
not too long ago.

:::

Broken Mind

Broken fragments of a mind so polluted it poisons all thoughts to the touch of each ridge mazing through these fingertips.

Whispering voices scurry through the corridors of the abandoned & cobwebbed trails with no breadcrumbs leading the way back to the sanity lost somewhere along the borders of deranged psychosis.

Doctors contribute to the madness with their mocktails of placebos, impersonating antidotes that'll shed some light into the darkness of these fucking atomized brain waves waving in the delusional comforts of feeling the madness—
being lifted,
lifted,
being lifted,
lifted,
being—
lifted like it was all a glitch of the mind but no, not really; the only glitch was not embracing the unbalanced teeter-totter of the bipolar absurdities whispered softly into the lips of these nerve endings directing the traffic of my actions into the schizophrenic tendencies murking my mind like sewage through a needle point sieve.

::::

I wish I had the ability to turn back time and change some of the decisions I made, several times over, but boy, oh boy, would I want to relive some of these moments all over again.

I would go back to when I was chasing a high in India, a high that took away the PTSD of my past and my feeling of loneliness. I chased it so hard, I forgot these unknown lands had their own set of laws.

I forgot, I was the foreigner attempting to travel these unknown lands as if the curvy roads leading to the heart of it, were not foreign to me. I chased this high until the soles of my feet had worn out the welcome signs at the borders I was attempting to cross.

I took for granted every little bit of kindness given to me, underappreciated it, and demanded for more. But my demands fell on rejection and so I was forced to turn back to the crumbled walls I built around my dilapidated kingdom.

Once I found my way back home, I decided I would bury my sorrows, just behind the gates of my domain. There I found snowy white mountains, where I'd go down the slopes, and end up swimming down by the rivers at the banks of my drunkenness with no lifeguard on duty.

There I found a shark circling the waters of my soul, desiring to take me in all for itself, and devour me until there was no longer a drop left of who I truly am in this existence, until I found myself awake enough to swim away from these poisoned waters and dig my way back into the confines of my four padded walls.

Tired of allowing these four walls to dictate to me, that I am the prisoner they've acquired each time I found myself defeated by the mental wars waging in my head, I walked out on them. I allowed this broken heart of mine to find a yellow brick road, which did not lead me to a wish granting wizard, but instead found a pig that would pull me out of the sty I trudged in, and directed me south to warmer lands of impassioned fires, only found in Cuba.

Once there, the pig introduced me to a high so good, my soul was enraptured by the flames of my addiction. I almost buried my soul within the pipe dreams of this high, only because of its promise to me.

The source of my addiction promised me, all its love so long as I kept the veil of secrecy, over my eyes whenever the flames burned hot enough, to burn away all doubts I would have about its malignant high.

After several attempts to sober up, I finally found the strength and rolled down the window to throw the pipe out on the side of the road.

Once sober, I fixated my eye on my surroundings, and let another muse captivate the lens of my addictions. I moved forward and let time move out from deserted lands, full of falsities, and constant abandon, each time the high wore off. And when the high wore off, I landed in Colombia, where they served *tres golpes* on a daily because that coke hit like a charm when needing to replace the past.

I followed curvy roads of dirt, painted in gold, leading to the Fountain of Youth. I drank from the fountain every time I tipped it over enough, to drown in its elixirs and drown me it did.

I drowned myself in all the waves, letting them carry me back and forth, and off the security I'd find at the shores of my sanity. But sanity would never be there for me to graze upon, because these four walls of insanity have reclaimed their lonely patient who succumbed to the limits created by my mind, because you are only limited by the limits you create, right?

At the end of the day, nothing can be changed, but I can still change the ending of this story.

But hold on, while I light up my next high.

⁝⁝⁝

Unpadded

I'm tired of being alone,
surrounded by four walls
that are not even padded
to soften the blow of solitude;
walls that reverberate with
every single thought of the
loneliness erupting from
within the ventricles of
my staled heart.
Explosive thoughts
full of emptiness,
in their acidic words
flowing to destroy
the small amount of sanity
left behind & roaming,
playing hide & seek
within the abandoned estate
of my putrid mentality
because these unpadded walls
do nothing to buffer
the feast of jeers
invading my heart.

⁝⁝⁝

Learning Again

I'm learning to live in my own skin
and on my own,
with this heavy heart of mine
that's been turned to stone.

Sadness wreaks
havoc thru my soul
and my body will
soon pay death's toll.

Though I try hard to break free
from this sadness,
nothing is able to silence the madness
within me.

A depression
so infused into my skin,
the sorrow is visible
even on my dirty grin.

Solitude has placed
a suffering burden on me
taking away a happy
future I once used to see.

For once this grief has
burned thru my existence
nothing will be left of me
in any consistence.

Left only to roam,
in a ghostly remembrance
a broken spirit
of brokenhearted transcendence.

::::

Head Case

I'm a head case full
of poisonous retentions
drowning in my quagmired past,
unable to free myself
from this massive puddle of shit
I'm desperately trying
to pull myself out of;
before I succumb to the aberrations
shredding my sanity into confetti
that's swept away with the past
as the future arrives.
And you,
you're here
reaching out for my hand
to pull me out of this endless abyss
that is my mangled mind,
with a promise in your eyes
to heal all of my wounds
without leaving any *cicatrices*.

:::

Journey

This journey man... it's hard as fuck but nobody said it would be easy. Nobody told me I'd be given it all on a tin platter plated in fool's gold that would melt at the mere touch from the acidic ridges on my fingertips.

Nobody told me, I'd be smiling while suppressing these hot fucking tears bubbling up from behind these boiling eyes and tainted with these bloody bipolar emotions I have wrapped in the depths of my depression.

Nobody told me, I'd feel my heart heal time after time with the delusion of having come across some notion of love only to have it plundered through the grinder of some god's savage pranks played on my mind.

Nobody told me, one night stands would be the equivalent of lonely nights wrapped in empty sheets stained with cum full of desires for a happier tomorrow and the sweat of forgotten yesterdays from the various unrecognizable bodies who have taken a brief tour of this life of mine; faces with blank smiles and sparkling eyes holding not a single goddamn expression with the warmth of this thing people call love.

Nah man, this journey has been fucking hell and without there being any damn shortcuts, sometimes I feel like just calling it a day and cutting this fucking trip short but, fuck man, ain't nothing of a quitter in me, so I continue trudging along the pitfalls of this fucking journey without looking back except to see how far I've come along and to wish some of these folks I've left behind would've chosen to stay the course with me; or at the very least, that one of these mu'fuckas would've given me a fucking light.

:::

You came into my life only to masturbate your ego & see how far it would go, before I drowned in your cum-soaked lies. Hung me out to dry in the sun and let the sun burn through my soul like your fake love burned through my heart. All I ask of you now is to please release my heart from the tourniquet of misery it has confined itself to for still being in love with you. I called you the love of my life, didn't I? Fuck, I did, didn't I?

But the love of my life turned out to be a fraud, claiming to love me the same in return, but you fucking lied; you fucking lied. You always kept me at a distance and only flew down to play with your prey when you needed to entertain yourself with the broken heart I've kept hidden within the rotten cavities of my chest for so long, and I let you in; I fucking let you in.

What a mistake it was to give you the key to the only delicate part of my being, only to have you open the doors, and destroy everything within the walls I had built up to protect myself. You took for granted your admission into my heart and crushed it with your lies and unkept promises; promises only made to keep me at bay, but for how long?

How long did you think I would go on accepting them all, without putting up a fight for your heart in its entirety? A battle fought for something never intended to be given to me at all or ever.

And though deep down inside of this beaten soul, I knew it would be a losing battle, I just had to accept it and let you go. And so, I did, I let you go on the side of the road where you supposedly buried your past too.

⁝⁝⁝

I was sitting at the bar when you saw me dressed in my flannel over a hoodie. On one side of me was an older man, not past his fifties in a raincoat, over a black turtleneck, slicked back fields of grey and intellectual glasses, black like my soul. To the other side of me, a younger man in his forties, with a mind fed through an alcohol infused grinder.

Cut off for the night he begs for a last drink, but constant denials leave him resigned to just sit there sipping on an empty glass, trying to suck out the air from the glass he's wrapped his drunken heart in. Leather Jacket collar up silver fox running across his scalp, and you sitting there, beside him, not giving any attention to his existence, but you notice mine.

Leather jacket sees you and attempts to sing you his broken melody, but it sounds like an out of tune piano that's needed to be tuned up for the past twenty years. He finally gives up, and gets up to walk away, and as soon as he's out of sight, you approach me, "Hey love, want to buy me a drink?".

"Sure, what're you 'aving?"

"I'll take a Stella"

I order your drink and pass it to you, and before I can say another word you get up, and say, “Here babe, now shut up, and let’s go”.

I turn around and see Leather Jacket leaning on the chair behind me. Well, ain’t that a bitch? Well, *fuck* can I do, but finish up my drink, and get the fuck out? I will continue my search for you again, tomorrow night, somewhere else.

:::

I see you there and just don't believe it's fair, all shattered and broken into shards of sadness. I knew I'd find you here my heart, at the bottom of this empty glass.

"Bartender, 'nother round please!"

Let's fill this sucka up and drown in my acidic sorrows this eternal heart of mine. Wipe these cold tears off my beaten soul and cleanse the blood off these mangled thoughts. Help me wash away these memories, movies played over and over in my head, like a video running on a never-ending loop, replays of all the worst times in my life,

"Bartender, 'nother round!"

Help me wash away the repressed memories of all the times I was abused, all the heartache injected right into my lifeless heart, and help me cleanse this polluted mind of mine, full of negative thoughts, wanting nothing else but to end it all; including this so-called smile on my fucking face.

:::

Faked feelings,
meant to cover up
a reality we do not desire.
Faked feelings,
meant to sequester solitude
and store it amongst
the shards of our
broken hearts forever.
Faked feelings,
meant to bandage old wounds
but the scars remain
and so does the loneliness
as long as these feelings
are faked;
but for once
let's pretend
this love is real
and not something
faked for companionship.

:::

I don't want to wake up tomorrow;
I want the loneliness
to wrap me up
in its arms,
like saran wrap
and vacuum out
all the oxygen
from every single cell
in my body,
because my mind
has already gone comatose
and my heart
has lost its drumming
from constant heartbreaks
and now lays dormant
at the heels of death
begging for entry
to the heavens
that await
past this life,
because
it's been nothing
but hell here.

Lived

[Devil spelled backwards]

CEDRIK O. WALLACE

ABOUT THE AUTHOR

Cedrik O. Wallace, Whittier College graduate and an Educator for the Los Angeles Unified School District in Los Angeles, California, is a published poet and self-published author who has recently joined the Magesoul Publishing family. His writing is simple and powerful as they come from a place of darkness and brightness. He was inspired to write in 2014 after his battle with cancer, where he nearly died and missed a year of work. It was in the same year that Cedrik began to share his writings, thoughts, and quotes on Instagram under the username @poeticsoldier [fighting cancer with poetry]. He had several poems published in various publications and went on to become a Top 100 Inspirational Instagrammer in 2017. Cedrik currently has two books available on Amazon. 'Why I Cry Burgundy Tears' is a memoir about his journey with cancer and 'It's My Write' is a collection of poetry and thoughts revolving around surviving cancer, self-love, relationships, social injustice, racism, education, and family.

Connect with Cedrik on social media:

@poeticsoldier
@booksbypoeticsoldier

@cedrikwallace
@booksbycedrik

Foreword

This chapter gives a descriptive account of Cedrik Wallace's truths revolving around the pain endured while surviving Multiple Myeloma, a blood cancer.

Each piece paints a picture detailing the symptoms of the cancer, the side effects of the various treatments, and the physical and mental state of life during and after cancer.

You will feel these words of strength and inspiration. Cedrik considers this chapter to be, "a spin off" to his debut book, Why I Cry Burgundy Tears.

'Lived' is a collection of poetic writings that portrays the cancer as being the devil who lived inside of Cedrik. It is what propelled Cedrik's will to fight which also lived inside of him.

"The pain was a different kind of pain...
I can't really describe it."

- excerpt from 'Why I Cry Burgundy Tears'

⁝⁝⁝

Read me.
I'm based on a true story.
The current chapter
is very telling.
You might be inspired.

:::

Caregiver Lives Matter

Dear cancer,

Why is it that you do, what you do?
To whomever you choose.

Mothers, fathers,
sisters, brothers,
sons, daughters,
and so on.

How much more of this
should we have to take?
The stress intake.
The lingering heartache.

It hurts. It's suffocating.
It's scary. It's restless.
Just give the message
you're attempting to deliver.
Fuck beating around the bush
and causing all this fuss.

I'm a survivor
but in this letter to you,
I'm asking on behalf
of a caregiver.

:::

Inside Effects

I'm a nervous wreck
and my hands shake.
A pounding headache
tied to a digestive ache.
Bouncing off the walls
as my heart races.
Trapped inside
is all one can take.
The bowel is moving
but not at the right pace.
The hinting growl
is not soothing
and attempting to escape
is the desire.
Oh wait!
It finally transpired but
again and again.
Followed by a short-lived
boost of energy.
Seeping through pores
are flashes of my inner fire.
All over I'm cramping
and the fatigue's got me crabby.
You can see in these words
that chaos is what
side effects bring me.

:::

My Backbone

I have brittle bones
and that's a fact.
I've lost nearly three inches
in my height
due to fractures in my back.
However,
I continue to stand strong.
What cancer didn't count on
was me having a spine
made of loved ones.

⁝⁝⁝

Medicine Bottle

I'm consumed by it.
Stuck inside.
Waiting for the cycle's end.
Being the last one
at the bottom drags
as the others are popped.
Feeling the effects
of the rattled bottle.
Every twist of the lid
exudes pain.
When finally swallowed
there is a sigh of relief
yet the suffering
starts all over
as the cycles never end.

:::

Tomorrow

I thought I was
in charge today
but the fatigue
has taken that away.
With that I'm okay
because I've learned
through this journey
that the good days
outweigh the bad days.

⁝⁝⁝

To Understand Fatigue

Imagine walls from all sides
moving in on you.
With your arms you attempt
to hold them off.
Only to rid yourself of any little energy
you may have had.
Overpowered and crushed
your limbs bust.
Weakness and anxiety take over.
Mentally and physically.
You lose all control and simply fold.
Just like the walls.
Your eye lids weigh heavier
than any regular tiredness and sleepiness.

:::

Hurt So Good

It hurt so bad!
That's when I realized
that the ***devil lived*** inside.
At first, I tried to
speak it out of existence
however, the devil
was being resistant.
A week later,
I was near dead in the hospital.
Asking myself, "Why me?"
fell on deaf ears
like some lame riddle.
A month later I broke away
from his killer grasp.
The joke was on him
as I walked out with the last laugh.

⁝⁝⁝

My Office

It's not what you see
when you walk in.
A museum of sorts.
Walls of structural integrity.
A dose of reality
tied in with a sense of immortality.
A color scheme that screams diversity.

Walk in and take a seat.
Sit in my chair for a while.
You will see
an arrogant wink
and a smile in disguise
once I've allowed you a glimpse
into the adversity I've survived.

Actually, I'm confident
after weakening some tough times.
A further scope into your own mind
may be inspired
after my purpose has been made clear
and growth you will endure.

:::

It's What You Gain

Emotions spill like pouring down rain
Washing away what you can.
Treating scars as stains.
Gradually they fade into some far distance
yet never really erasing the pain.
Using it to plant roots
as a foundation for your next move.
From there you get into
a much-needed rhythmic groove.
Falling into place is everything
just right like deep puddle waves
in their outward moves.
Your surrounding soiled seeds
absorb the drops from that mental storm
only to take from it, life, in order to bloom.

⁝⁝⁝

Lethal Injection

Living life as if
you're on death row.
Allowing your demons
to eat away at your soul.
It will be a lethal way to go.
So, grab the devil
by the horns
and take self-control.

:::

Stand Up To Cancer

Let us be aware.
The answer is out there.
They know where.
The greedy just don't care
because it's not about
the people's welfare.
It's all about filling their own
pockets off of gimmicks.
So, for them, exposing a cure
will always be off limits.
So, it's on us to start a revolution
against this epidemic.

⁝⁝⁝

Writing The Hurt

Word for word spilling
out of an introvert.
Speaking as they're written
to rid the hurt,
instead of a verbal convert.
Decades of selfishly
keeping truths to myself.
Thanks to cancer,
now I've opened up.
Allowing my emotions to erupt.
Unselfishly baring my soul
in hopes that the pain will fold.

:::

At The End

Cancer is the devil
but I am the rebel.
Defying him will tell
how its prayer that I've felt.

Fearing only the one above
because the evil below
will never know such love
that my praying warriors show.

Killing many in his path
and striking fear beyond,
I will escape his wrath,
being one of God's strongest,
when it's all said and done.

:::

Fight 'til Death

Spell ***devil*** backwards
and you get lived.
Just as the devil did
inside of me and as
I lived life moving forward.

I will have lived
a beautiful life
having lived out
my purpose.

Unfortunately for Mr. Devil,
until then,
I plan to stick around
and be a burden.

He may get what he wants
in the long run.
However, I will not have just
taken it laying down.
I will have gone round for round,
bout for bout, and risen
after each knockdown

The Aftermath

KRISTIN L. PROVENZANO

ABOUT THE AUTHOR

Kristin Provenzano was born and raised in Akron, Ohio. She started writing at a young age and had her first poem published in high school. Falling into poetry as a way to heal from the toxic relationships she had been in over the years, Kristin was inspired to write about what she'd endured, hoping that by sharing her own journey, it may help others deal with their own experiences, and realize they are not alone in this world. Kristin encourages people to know it's okay to talk about what has happened in their life and that we are all in this, together. Becoming a Magesoul Publishing Home Author in 2019, her debut collection, 'The Wilted Walls' was released in January 2020 and is available on Amazon.

Connect with Kristin on social media:

 @kristin_l_provenzano

I was crawling on the ground
Everything finally got to me
Couldn't remember
Anything anymore
The reflection in the mirror
Was not my own
I grabbed on to the sheet
To pull myself up
Only to lose grip
Nothing else felt familiar
The only thing I knew was
How cold this floor was

:::

I made up this illusion
In my head of us
We were fine
The screams got louder though
Eyes got redder
The words we couldn't take back
Bruises that could no longer stay hidden

:::

My phone went off
It was you
You left a voicemail
But I didn't want to listen to it
You had a way with your words
That would lead me
Right back to you
To those stomach pains
Headaches
Solitary confinement

:::

You cried like it was the end of the world
Begging me not to leave
How many times did I cry to you before?
Wanting you to just hear me
To show you gave a fuck
Now since the door is opened
That small bag in the closet is finally being used
I need to stay
Hear you out
You get how I once felt
To be left alone
Your choices do have consequences
It was the end of us

:::

This was the third time
You walked out on me
After that I became
Dead on the inside
Everything ran dry
Even my tears

⁝⁝⁝

I loved you so much
That I lost myself
A thin
Fragile woman
Stuck with the chaos in her head
That you put there
Doubting every thought she had
About your treatment of her
Making the fault her own in the end
That’s what was left in front of you

:::

You left behind
That bottle of good scotch
I kept staring at it
While drinking a glass of red wine
At the dinner table
Which I now sit at alone
I told myself
It's trouble if you taste it
I never did listen though
After the first drop touched my tongue
It was all you
I brought you back
When I so desperately needed
To forget you

:::

She didn't want it to end
He was her life
The air she breathed
Her hero that you read about in books
He never saw her like that
She was just another girl
Someone to have between the sheets
He had too many options
Just another mark on his wall
Another used up condom

:::

I covered up my eyes
With my sunglasses
You could see the pain in them
I wasn't ready for questions
The input
Was over talking about me
About us
In this moment
I just wanted to act like
We never existed
In the first place

:::

You needed your time away
Time to think
Figure us out
That time away though
Was you exploring
Seeing what else was out there
To see if you could find better than me
I never was enough for you
I never would be

:::

I tried to pick up all my pieces up
There were some I couldn't find
I searched all over
Realizing you took some of me with you
With you never wanting me
To be whole again

⁝⁝⁝

The imprint in my bed
Became bigger
The stench of cigarettes
Became stronger
And the dampness on the floor
From my tears
Started making it impossible
To walk across

::::

After a while
I didn't care if you were around anymore
I was so used to it being just me
That when you made yourself present
It was like a stranger
Appeared

:::

We were nearing the end
I could see it
The airbags wouldn't deploy this time
There was nothing left to be salvaged
Lies and tears everywhere
Walking away barely intact

Embracing My Fears

ADRIC CENERI

ABOUT THE AUTHOR

Adric Ceneri is an artist, poet, writer, and author. He was born in Mexico and lived there during his childhood. He was raised in the coasts of the Pacific Ocean with his parents up to the age of five, and when his parents separated, he had to endure and survive the consequences of his parents' poor life choices. The majority of his poetry reflects his subsequent pain and suffering. He writes about his sexuality and the events that marked him throughout childhood and the difficulties he faced when he was growing up. Ceneri often writes with a rebellious heart through his poetry, expressing his emotions and always remaining true to who he is as an artist. As a poet and writer, he transmits his feelings and embodies his transgressions in magical wordplays truly transforming pain into art. Adric's four journals and his books 'Walking Towards Happiness' and 'Caminando hacia la Felicidad', are available on Amazon. Marketing Manager and Home Author for Magesoul Publishing, he is also the creative genius behind the cover of 'It Hurts'. His books 'The Remains of a Human' and 'Los Restos de un Humano' will be available June 2020.

Connect with Adric on social media:

 @adricceneriwrites  @adricceneri

 www.adricceneri.com  @ceneriadric

Despite It All

If only I could swallow my pride,
if only you knew
how much I needed you in my life.
That I can never forgive you
for having moved away from my world,
because I was the boy
and you were my father, the adult.

You left without saying goodbye,
without a farewell,
while I stayed in your misery, in your past.
I always tried to fit into society;
a mistake I'll regret for the rest of my life.
I had no one in my childhood,
nobody who could understand the pain
eating me up in the inside.

I always fought to be accepted
in one and a thousand ways,
but for being different
the only thing I ever received were bruises.
I found myself without family
and with many doubts about who I was,
and loneliness showed me
the pain of darkness growing inside my heart.

It hurts so much to remember
how much I tried to be liked,
all I wanted was to see you proud of me
but you pushed me aside.

It hurts even more to know
that for you I was always a hindrance,
you were only a sperm donor,
who never earned the title father and that's a fact!

Only I know how many times
you despised me coldly,
it makes me angry and all I can wish for,
is to remove your genes from my blood.

My life didn't need your misery,
I already had enough of that,
what a pity that I was for you
only the revenge against your wife.

You thought she would suffer
if you took me away to unknown lands,
but I was the one who suffered
with promises that I never saw realized.

How much could you have loved me
if I am in pieces today
because of your damn lies?

Antonio, you were so egotistical
and ***it hurts*** that you buried me
under all your bitter hatred and shattered pride.

I couldn't give you more than what I gave,
my heart is broken beyond repair
because you never valued what I've felt.
I never mattered to you in any way.

I can't forgive you for using me,
and I hope you never find forgiveness for your sins.
I'm not proud to be the son of a misogynist,
and please forget me, erase me from every memory.

I was a child and ***it hurts*** to know you never cared,
I never received love from you but I turned out okay.

For you, I was and always will be
nothing more than a bad investment,
but all your hate one day will consume you
and it will be your own destruction and punishment.

I can't feel sorry for your petty soul
because you have no love,
but still, I wish for nothing more
than what you deserve.

⁝⁝⁝

It Was Always Like This

You were the reason I smiled every morning waking up,
but those dreams didn't stay and broke me apart.
Now I wake up looking for my mother at night,
and awake I realize I am no longer that child,
and that our stolen time won't ever come back.

I am no longer that kiddo who's got a broken heart,
looking for love and shelter
but only found himself alone in the dark.

Only my pillow knows about my night torments,
my pillow, who dries my tears that have no affection,
and lets me embrace it to forget my desolation.

Only the silence and solitude know me well,
they, who've always dragged me far away,
and repeat to me that it is okay to cry all of my pain.

It hurts me to say that I have many regrets,
to say that I only have wounds and deep pain,
wounds that I wish to erase from my heart one day.

Hope has always failed me a thousand times,
so naive, I believed in Hope and gave it
a second chance,
expecting this time, the story would be different,
expecting to alas find true love for a long time.

Out of my eyes salted tears well up,
and voices emerge out of my mind,
they ask me to let my vein's blood run free,
they want me to leave my lifeless body asleep.

They want me to run away from this world,
they say that no one will notice I'm gone.
They offer me happiness, to where I'll go,
they say I deserve an end for what I've done.

My broken body is turning cold,
but my dreams await wrapped in hope.
It hurts to know that I couldn't do more.
My broken dreams are for me, now a tale,
and slowly I'm going away with the darkness.

:::

Help Me

God, please help me stand up,
help me to take the next step...
Give me the strength to get up,
to understand my life and to accept myself as I am.

You know well how much I have walked,
the times I have stumbled in the dark,
how much I have crawled, and for what?
If I remain indecent among sins and lies...
But who can teach my stubborn heart,
that feelings are not vain at all?
Who can show me I was wrong,
that the fury of my hate, poisoned my soul?

I would like to keep trying but ***it hurts***,
I feel a prisoner of my own humiliation,
my supplication and my sadness,
my life has become a routine of torture
and endless grievances tempting my madness,
it hurts so much that I am getting used to it,
getting used to the misery I endured at your hand.

God! Slap me, beat me and yell at me,
but please wake me up from this nightmare.
You, who knows my qualities and my imperfections;
you, who knows what I deserve
and what I am not deserving of.
And if I was paying for something,
I swear, I already paid more than what I owed.

:::

Embracing My Fears

I just don't get it.
How far will we get?
This cruel life and me.

I'm lost in this hell.
My eternal sorrows feel timeless.
How can I free my heart from history?

I no longer wish to run away from my early burial.
I want to finally admit it for a moment.
Now that ***it hurts*** as I drown myself in alcohol.

I want to tell my most sinister secret,
vent the deepest of all my agonies.
Being able to observe my reflection
at the precise moment when I set my anger free.

I am embracing my fears.
Dismantling all the horror they made me feel.
I'm forgiving myself for what I did,
and looking for the redemption that I need.

It is too late to learn, to simply live,
I understand I never knew what it meant to exist.
I no longer want to lie or hide my tears.
I just want to embrace the fear inside of me.

I want to let my fear dissolve along with me.
I want to feel myself fall apart finally,
and run towards death feeling the cold over me.
Letting go of the life I never wanted to live.

I'm embracing my fears,
facing everything I ever feared.
I'm facing the end of my mortality,
this is what I want,
it hurts but I will go through with it.
I am ready for my last breath
and this shall be my last heartbeat.

:::

Broken Mirror

I'm not going to take any hopes on this trip,
I will only carry my tears that spill at my feet.
I will take with me those rejections of love,
the direct abuse to my heart and soul,
as I get to leave behind a compassionless world.

I'm not going to take any memories of our love,
I will only carry my broken wishes and loss.
I know you will miss me, but I can't come home,
and you will seek me but I won't be anywhere,
because I'm going to the mirrored universe.

I'm going to turn my world like flipping a page.
Changing the ink of every word I ever said,
typing the pain and hurt in every inch of my flesh
so, I can get to remember this ache that I felt.

I'm going to enjoy the melancholy because ***it hurts,***
I'm going to suffer my heartache without affection.
And when I find my sadness filled with rejection,
my wide eyes will get to weep my desolation.

I intend to lose our happy memories,
and I plan to never return from this odyssey,
my journey to the other side of the mirror will be,
the ending of the painful story we lived.

It hurts to know that you never cared for me,
and that is why from your life I shall disappear,
in the early morning as the rain washes over me,
and my reason cleanses from this tragic dream.

You are the one I will forget,
by leaving our story behind.
Today my heart will finally rest,
by traveling to the other side.

And as my broken mirror gets to shred my sins,
my pain will perish dissected, piece by piece,
and I won't remember my pagan memories,
and you will die one day never knowing
that I have forgotten you permanently.

:::

Destroy Me

Destroy me with your words as I feel how ***it hurts***,
today that you still control me as you do.

Destroy me before you run away,
before you leave,
finish me at once and end my suffering.

Destroy me along with the memories of our past,
so that I won't remember you in the time to come.
By then I won't even be a memory for you,
I will die in pain, that aches in truth.

Destroy me,
finish me and let me see
how your hands murder me,
destroy me, finish me
and let me savor this pain as ***it hurts***
while sipping my last alcoholic drink…
So that I make a toast for what we lived,
for the permanent damage you inflicted in me.
Destroy me,
your unfaithful love today can no longer be.

Destroy me but don't lie to me,
I know you've been cheating,
and you have no idea
how these thorns of betrayal cause me agony,
how bad my heart aches,
it hurts to feel how it's dying...

Destroy me before saying you have to go,
that you're leaving,
kill me completely and allow me to feel ***it hurts,***
I want to feel absolutely nothing.

Destroy me along with our story
once and for all,
because I know that for you,
I was never worthy.
Today you leave me without you
while away you go.

Destroy me,
finish me and erased from my mind
your memories,
destroy me and finish me.
I want to be done with this story.

Destroy me…
Because in your luggage
are my smiles you packed away,
and all you left was my aching,
this pain, flowing through my every cell.

Destroy me because ***it hurts***,
because today I'm not even a shadow
of the person I was yesterday.

:::

Drawing My World's End

Therefore, and as much as I want to forget,
only my old years I have managed to tread,
waiting only to eliminate the fear inside my head...

My Hope has grown tired wrapped in Depression,
I am tired of looking for Forgiveness in the floor,
and I can't find the solution to my pain in words.

I have swallowed my pain of subtle bitterness,
waking up crying for not wanting to live anymore.
For the heavens ***it hurts***
not having a reason to remain in this world.

Depression does not leave me;
it has clung onto my soul.
My Anger is filled with hatred, it's beginning to burn,
and its hurtful thorns cut my mortality
painfully and slow...

I imagined my end would happen at dawn
on that bluish and starry morning,
where I will let myself go,
under clear skies filled with joyful thoughts
and the moonlit reflection over the sea
captivating my aching heart...

I want to believe
that this is the only way out of this life,
so I can finally set myself free
on this cold dawn in a wet tide,
under the deep blue sea
as it drowns me sinking away my life...

:::

He Raped Me

I had just turned eleven in the year 1999,
I was sleeping and he woke me up.
One of the most violent moments of my life,
I was used like a disposable rag.

I was only a child, lost in the dark
and he was a pedophile searching to fuck
an animal who didn't care to take pleasure by force,
he hurt my body and broke my spirit for the first time.

He took me by force under his arms,
he tore my soul and shredded my heart.
He didn't understand the physical pain he caused,
he didn't care for the tears in my eyes…
I said no but he still didn't stop.

I was alone and I suffered a lot,
I screamed, yelled and cried.
I fought him but my strength wasn't enough,
and no one came to my rescue
while he spread my cheeks apart.

He forced himself on top of me,
a wild animal in heat…
He was so strong and violent,
He punched me twice, to make me stop resisting him…
and I felt the pain as he thrusted himself inside.

I kept sobbing trying not to cry,
filled with fear… I was afraid,
I was trapped under his hands holding me down.

He was nineteen…
A perpetrator who marked me with violence.

He came, he came inside…
He finished and left me in state of shock.
My mind was floating in thoughts of suicide.
I felt worthless, and dirty, I wanted to die…
I felt helpless and angry with God,
I felt broken and I thought of taking my life…
But I didn't know how!!!
I didn't know how…

I was raped for being an effeminate boy,
I was abused because I was alone,
because I had no one who cared.

It hurt back then and it still hurts,
this marked me, it marked my childhood,
it is something I can't simply forget,
and this scar still hurts even though it has healed.

:::

Escaping Death

Walking on foreign space,
breathing stolen oxygen.
Living the life, I wasn't supposed to get.

I feel struggle inside my chest,
knowing I am here and not in hell.
This is the burden I must bear.

I am breathing borrowed breaths,
feeling the ticking of time…
in every heartbeat my heart makes.

Cheating life and escaping death.
Running always away from her,
maybe this time I should run towards her.

That's the anecdote
that traps me in every daybreak.

Waking up tired of always being prepared
always ready, one step ahead…
and I wonder why I can't stop running,
even if ***it hurts***, even if it is just for one day.

:::

Returning to The Point of Breaking

Some memories are a bliss
other are the nightmares I lived.
Can't help to not wake up crying
when I see my remorse and my fears.
It hurts to feel the guilt inside me,
the shame of everything I never fixed.

Feeling my pain, I ran out of thoughts,
every night always fighting my sleep.
It hurts to feel lost in every fear,
and is tough to survive my burning dreams.

Never knowing how long it will be,
always waiting and time takes its time to leave.
The uncertainty of not knowing,
eats away every last part of my sanity.
It's a constant challenge inside me,
my mind is going insane feeling these agonies.

And as the cold wind slaps my face,
I hear the birds singing sad melodies.
I can smell the snow as it falls over me.
I am waiting, waiting on time as I taste my tears.
Can't wait no longer in this awful place of my birth,
I keep telling myself, "this is just a nightmare,
and soon you'll wake up from this awful dream."

But then I wake up and ***it hurts*** far more
knowing it wasn't a bad dream.
Knowing that I am back here,
that I have returned to the place that broke me,
back in the place where I lost everything.
A vivid reminder of my tragedies,
I try to stay strong but I feel the weight of my guilt.

This guilt... ***it hurts***...
like heavy lead sinking in my every dark memory.
It's the way people see me in the light of day…
the reason why I don't want to go outside and play.
The obscure darkness calls out to me,
it's the demons I carry inside of me,
they keep breaking my spirit as I keep them contained,
and I don't know how much longer I can bare my pain.

It hurts... it pains me...
I ran away from this place decades ago...
How did I end back here?
I feel lonely in this third world.

I feel alone in this hell once more,
never thought I could ever feel these thorns.
But I feel them and they're sharper than before,
they're crushing my shattered and aching soul.
I feel loneliness get heavier as ghosts haunt me,
and I can only sit and watch it dissipates my joy.

Somehow, I don't feel worthy,
I don't feel that I am enough on my own.

It was terrifying thinking of being alone,
but here I am living away from my home,
from my husband and my loving world.
I find myself in the darkness, unloved.

I am in pain and filled with madness,
I am in rage and in the darkness,
you cannot blame me for sinning again…
like I have done…

I no longer want to be this victim in sadness,
for I want to at last feel some kindness,
I don't want to feel the hate that I have hosted.
This confusing psychotic emptiness,
it turns my madness into a ticking bomb.

Tears pouring down unresolved,
burning like fire with the rage I thought gone.
Is the hatred I carry and cannot let go.
Is the darkness inside my very soul,
the rage in my chest breathing like an animal,
burning me in pain for my tragic loss,
I can't stop feeling shame and remorse,
for it is triggered by this place I hate the most.

Emotionless

ERICA VARELA

ABOUT THE AUTHOR

Erica Varela was born and raised in Perth Amboy, NJ and currently resides in Los Angeles, Ca. In addition to writing, she enjoys a staff position with one of the most successful music record labels in the world, WMG. Staying true to her passion for writing as well as music. She is accredited for co-producing and composing music for LA's Underground music scene, and has fronted many bands, including her own. Joining Magesoul Publishing as a Home Author last year, Erica is heavily focused on pursuing her current adventure and love, Poetry. Since joining the Magesoul team, she has released the beautiful collections "Ruby" and "Timeless Depths" and re-released her debut book "Honey". 2020 is set to launch an entirely new collection. Erica's books can be purchased at www.ericavarela.com or via Amazon.

Connect with Erica on social media:

 @writerericavarela

 www.ericavarela.com

:::

The Poet

I'm not one to cry.
I'm not one to be put on a pedestal.
I am an imbalanced sense of self.
Like an old timepiece
that needs rewinding,
A doormat that's used to being walked on,
now weathered.
I am just the reflection
you make me out to be.
But I am neither nor.
Like a fish who drowns in water,
A breath that forgets to breathe,
A facade of what defines make believe,
I am what you see in my false semblance.

I am, my worst enemy.

:::

Not Your Fool Anymore

Share another lie
with me dear,
as you push me away.

Keep me a secret,
and silent I will be
in your bed.

Speak with your lips.
Your lies and crooked teeth.
Bright red face, coarse hair.

Tell me this time, is not the time.
For your snowed-in heart
no longer feels warmth.

What was once, twice;
and by the third time,
I will disappear.

:::

Reality

I sit here waiting
for the sun
to exist once again;
to fake a smile.

Tell everyone I'm ok.

When the truth is,
sitting on this cold porch at 4am,
I am drowning with the ocean
that lays miles away from my body.

Barely breathing.

Keeping my nose
above its waves.
I'm not manic, nor
am I depressed.

A “mixed state”.

Smoking lungs, inhaling cancer.
Void filler.
My gift to you?
A clock.

Tic Toc, Tic Toc.

Hands clicking.
Shows me
we've come to our end.
I once did love you. Never fully.

A stenciled shape, resembling a heart.

:::

Irrelevant Benefits

Room lights, low and dim.

At my desk where only I know where things lie.
Pen and paper in hand, minds a hovering surprise.

Been watching these colors,
as racing hours are an excuse to not be near.

What is here, hasn't been a phone call away
.... Again, I know, second was your choice.

My heart goes out to you –
and it beats, while I shatter.

:::

Little Louder

Describe to me again,
How you have NEVER felt a love like mine?

Tell me again, how much you want to feel me,
Hold me, I see you're afraid to lose me.

Now come closer…
How does it feel to dream of only me?

Choices you've made-
for your own comfort.

:::

Ending Days

We fell asleep drunkenly
on our last night.
I held you so tight
no loosening of arms.
The next morning
I awoke with your deadly words.
In a hurry, I rise up,
melancholy.
As I bleed to hear you say,
"Stay."
Wishing for your heart to speak-
You remained *silent.*

⁝⁝⁝

Editor

I have never needed your eyes.

For our story,
I was just another character
Playing her role;
as your girlfriend -
in your silent film.

⁝⁝⁝

Emotionless

I am overly dying in emotions
Kept inside –
void to voided-
overly have I become –
“emotionless”.

Haven’t I been hurt enough?

⁞⁞⁞

Spill On Me

I've always admired writers,
they who pour out their hearts,
before death.
I am an inkless pen,
I write each letter with blood stains.
Now, there's just blood across
my fitted sheets,
where I lay,
in dried ink.

Even Angels Fall

ANGELA MARIE NIEMIEC

ABOUT THE AUTHOR:

Angela Marie Niemiec is a poet who began writing as a way to express her deepest, darkest feelings. Inspired by strong connections, poetry is her way of bridging the gap between the lonely soul and pure human connection. It's that bond that is the key to opening her creative side; resonating with others is the bonus. Her first poem was published in an art book in Poland and subsequent ones appear in several other anthologies worldwide. Her premier book, "Once Around the Halo", published in 2019, is a collection of poems on a spiritual journey to find healing while battling chronic illness, loss and heartache. After falling into a deep depression, she used poetry as an escape from reality, but quickly found that words could truly bring healing. Heavily riddled with metaphor, she initially takes pain and turns it into something dark in her mind. However, when writing about the darkness, she has a way of still holding onto the light and you will see this in her poems. Instead of remaining in the grips of victimhood, she will raise you to empowerment.

Connect with Angela on social media:

 @angel_writer

⁙

Worn
paper thin
I never thought that you
would rip me apart
and tear me
to shreds.

:::

Hell Swallowed Heaven

Where have all the angels gone,
drained petals of their colors,
greyed rainbows scatter off to dust,
only echoes of a holy song,
where have all the angels gone?

One by one,
plucked from the earth,
some too soon, some by choice,
no holiness left, it's been destroyed,
an emptiness ensues this void.
Ripped from rattled rusty chains,
unbound feathers escalate,
up to the sky they were misled,
all the angels have now fled.

The balance tipped to dooms dark end,
fear is the only emotion undigested,
tears dried up by hell's dark heat,
appetite null, they force the feed.

Emotional swallows of the deepest shade of dread,
pure white wings are stained of red,
all the angels have been bled.

This was it,
the end of ends,
the devil arrived on the Plain of Esdraelon,
declaring to all an Armageddon.
This is what happened
when hell swallowed heaven.

:::

Drown

I can go down
to the depths in which you'd drown
and I'll drag myself
into the undertow
just to see how cold it is
in places with no light.

I can go down
and dance with the extremophiles
living under pressure
about to crack,
I can go down
to that place in your mind
a total self-attack,
I can go there
and not come back.

Throw me a line,
reel me in,
keep me on track,
don't let me go under too long,
because without you,
I would go down,
forevermore,
without you
I'd drown.

:::

Monsters Are Real

Becloud to vanish and drain to pass,
the lines that blur cross-fade to black,
glass hearts slip from hands loose grip,
crashing down on shattered ground.
From up in clouds to ocean's floor,
sends tsunami force on hostile shores,
swallowing souls of mortal sins,
pure black feathers have fallen
beneath the shadow of a raven's wing.
From the molt it sheds the lies,
deceit spreads seeds across fields of despise,
lost dreams roll downward,
to out of view,
there's nothing left of the 'me' you knew.
Splintered souls now set ablaze,
embody reflections of the devil's gaze,
into burning saltwater eyes,
into the blackest hearts of those you stole,
you took it all, and this you know.
Stare deep into the mirror of truth,
stare until you see it too…

Monsters are real,
they look just like you.

:::

The Devil Can Silence You *If You Let Him*

Drained.
Nothing left inside,
like a cup tipped upside-down,
striving for one last drop to roll from the edge,
but left disappointed,
because it's all gone,
dried up like a forgotten desert.
Dehydration crumbles away at my delicate petals,
the colors run dry,
no more dye,
the rainbows have all drained away,
faded to grey,
pushing my pencil harder only makes it break.
Maybe I'm almost dead,
or was it just the devil living inside my head,
whispering until I was silenced.
The quieter I became,
the more isolated I made myself,
the more recluse,
pushing everyone away,
only made me have more to say,
but I just don't know how to let it out.
I have so much to say,
but can't remove the tape.
He'd rather keep me *silent.*

:::

Lies Like Fire

Lies are as violent as fire,
ones of this type aren't put out
with something as simple as water.
Water is too transparent
for the opaque picture you painted
in a black sea of sins,
and you know your cunning words
cut right through my crisp white sails,
that you blew from your lungs of uncertainty,
like wind, you cast me out to sea,
and when you see me,
I'll just be a dot on your forgotten horizon.
I'll throw an anchor overboard,
but it won't sink far enough,
I'm on the deepest edge of reality
and your head in the astral cloud of deceit,
we couldn't be further apart.
I keep waiting for my anchor to hit sea floor,
to secure me to at least one safe place,
but I keep drifting,
further
and
further
.
.
away.

:::

Temporary

People always leave.
We're all human,
but why so temporary?
Pushed around
until pushed aside,
ignored,
forgotten,
abandoned.

How could you do this?

In the end,
you think you left me
with nothing,
but really,
I left you
with something more…

That hole in your heart
that nothing's been able to fill,
quite the way I once did.

:::

Walk Away

Strike the match and burn away
all the struggles that led you astray
nostalgia can suffocate,
tangled wires that spark when they connect,
blow the smoke away and evaporate,
dissipate and disconnect,
pull the plug,
there is no race,
no end to cross,
no one to compete with once you're gone…
Just echoes
and a long shiver of goosebumps
as it ends
with a
bang.

Go.
The gun says run,
but I choose to walk…
away.

Slow and steady wins the race.

⁝⁝⁝

Still on Fire

Bewilderment ran concentric circles,
dizzying cycles of phantasmal trance,
lost in the space and time continuum.
Can fire burn where gravity does not exist?
Crimson strewn petals trail a path to madness,
until utter exhaustion collapsed my infernal reflection
into the burning splash.

The water stilled into a placid mirror,
I saw my eyes,
wearing heavy lashes,
bear witness to the disintegration of ink and bone,
pushing my pen into the storm,
grinding friction until fires form…

The ones you constantly ignite in your mind.

They will never burn long enough
to melt the hands of time,
backward splashing discord into the depths,
disrupting lucid stillness,
rippled waves match the chaos.

⁝⁝⁝

Hell would invite you in,
but you can't swim
with the devil himself
You can't breathe
when the halo falls around your neck,
you can't cleanse the tar
from stained black wings,
you can't dig the earth
deep enough
to set me free.

Just cast me away
on a funeral pyre,
and burn me away
with every last piece
of my own
godforsaken poetry.

⁝⁝⁝

Far Fall

Part I: Some say the fall is the hardest part.

Jumping from cliffs to take the plunge
of the exit I always anticipate,
the fall will be far, but too near,
the sky will be falling inward,
all my memories sweeping over my face,
head rushes of mad blood boil the surface heights,
flushed cheeks drain to pale,
the life being sucked out in a single swift step,
knowing how hard the crash will be,
feeling the grips of anxiety,
maybe I will be the first to go,
I'll shoulder the blame,
wear it like a cape,
one that can hopefully save us all,
because I would never want to feel
all two hundred and six bones snapping in unison.
So with all my might, I'll take one step back,
to save the last true thing I have left to hold,
my sanity, safely cocooned within
my inevitable metamorphosis.

⁝⁝⁝

Part II: Grow your wings in the darkness of the fall,
you'll need them on your way down.

The power of a black hole
pulls at my mortal soul,
standing at the edge of the event horizon,
swirling inward gravitational acceleration.

Never let me go too far.
Never let me fall.

Powder my budding wings,
catch my whispered breath
beaming up to sparkling skies,
float me along in a rowing boat,
paddling stars from battling lashes,
because when the mass of the black hole
grasps the edge and won't let go,
only butterflies can escape
the darkness of a far fall.

⁝⁝⁝

Part III: When you whisper to the sky, it answers.

I fell asunder in a silent thunder,
caught in a net of self-doubt,
tangled in a web of confusion,
locked in a cell of disarray.
I let dissolution
eat away at my mind
like a buffet,
spread for the taking.
I accidentally let the demons in,
dangling the keys to the cellar door
right before their preying eyes,
gently holding a welcome sign
to darken my mind,
and feast they did.

I let them in,
and I let them win.

I let them feed and regurgitate
malevolence into my ears and eyes
until I nearly disappeared.

I let them in,
and I let them win.

I let them push me around,
push me away,
pull at my faith
and disintegrate my wings
until I was nearly invisible.

Mercilessly,
they watched me bleed,
pushing me closer to the end,
backing me to the final edge,
with nothing left,
no reason to be,
it was finally time to go.

Right before I took the plunge,
I looked up to the sky
and whispered, "*How far?*"
and the sky answered…

"If you let your demons catch you every time,
you'll never truly learn to fly."

:::

Double Knotted

The last day I was stepped on,
was the first day I learned
to double knot my laces.

My soul became worn so thin
from tiptoeing
around these insidious opinions.

With each step of the way,
for all the things
that I could never change,
I became undone;
dragging my soles along the ground,
my laces became more and more long,
until I dug my heels
into the depths of the dirt
and realized
it's time to heal.

It's time to pull myself up
from all the stompings,
from all the skinned knees
and hands that bleed,
it's time to tie it up
and tie it shut.

So, step on me no more
you won't,
I've learned to double tie loose ends tight,
and even though it's bound my heart in knots,
at least no longer will I fall
the next time
someone tries
to trip me.

⁝⁝⁝

P.S.

Never dim your light
for someone who can't handle
all of your brilliance.

Broken Pieces of Togetherness

ALEX LE'GARE

ABOUT THE AUTHOR

Alexander Le'Gare is an American Poet from Jacksonville, Fl. Having found a love for literature and art as an adolescent, Alexander began reading and writing poetry by the tender age of eight. He would go on to remain a poet in secret for many years, afraid of being misunderstood. However, his passion for creativity along with a desire to inspire poetically; he found himself unable to keep his craft silent and since he first performed at age fifteen, he has gone on to share his work via social media and various Poetry night venues. Equipped with a unique sense of rhythm and imagery, Alexander delivers his poetry like a painting. Mind-bending metaphors, accompanied by profound simplicity tend to make his work a pleasure to read. Now a Home Author for Magesoul Publishing, his insatiable drive to inspire and be inspired is ultimately what has landed him on the cusp of publishing his debut book titled, "The Side Effects of L. A Poetic Purge" scheduled to be released in 2020! The book is to be nothing short of a portal to which the reader is given the opportunity of veering into the mind and thoughts of this lyrical and storytelling author.

Connect with Alex on social media:

 @legare.monroe

⁝⁝⁝

Aldora

So I held your heart in one
Left your mind up for the taking
Should I ever find its depths to pierce
Tell me when it gets old

We found comfort in the quiet
Pulsating to the wire
Everything was felt aloud
In a labyrinth of silence

I knew nothing more than to breathe
Still air, is an exhale
Into my lungs you're launched
I take you in as my breach

Aldora, I feel you breaking by the ends
Let's hold it together 'til you say
There's no other way
This, is where it gets old

One you'll have had enough
I don't know which month it's under
But around the corner
Never felt closer

It's an end that's far from over
Beginning with a drag
Us two came to, heavy healings
What's another bag!

It's just that we hate it
In between those lines
We die in those spaces
Right between the eyes

I can honestly say I saw it coming
Too close for comfort
A windy wil'o wisp
Never far behind

Aldora? Are you listening still?
Are you far too educated for your listening skills?
Aren't you cramped against that cusp?

With just enough pressure
We're both held in place
Every line is for lynching
Every tear is a trace

Day breaks on your matte black brows
Your eyes kill whatever's left
The windows to the soul
Before it bit its way out

O' Aldora newness is a virtue
Unaffordable to us; poor souls
All we've got is enough
There's always each other

Understatements; overkill
Our tarantella in the balance
Watch me beat my dead heart
Until it gets old
And I reign
Over every regret.

:::

My Wings & Frivolous Things

I was merely the wind
Blowing through time
Shifting through space
Calmly, turnt fiercely
Through the day & night
Like a breezy-secret weapon
Built to yield the rain
When the air is fresh it shields from pain
And I graze your gashes
Like kisses blown on ashes

Toward the Sun
Which was me
I brought closure to clouds
Storms stayed astray
As I bathed you from grey
It feels like yesterday
Like everyday

Came a night, half a Moon; I was
Breaking my back to barely light the mist
While you squint on the tint of the trees
And you bleed from your sleeve hoarding hearts
In the sky I could spark
If I'm lucky
You could see me
In the stars; when it's dark

Cause the sky is out of space
That's why heaven was erased
And though I'm gone
Through counted days
And calendar stains

Of all that was missed
Every scar needs its kiss
Every Angel begs for wings
Amongst other frivolous things

:::

Beautifully Timed Weapons

Clocks are controlled
Yet time is on the loose
Your eyes are fixed
I'm broken by 6

Troubleshooter
You're trigger happy
One millimeter into measuring my mess
You press against my spine and tell me its 9

Impossible to stand a chance
Cause that one foot found a grave
If looks could kill I'd glance
But my face always plants in my hands

See, goodbyes are visible
Leaving wounds on display
Breath aborning by morning
You blow me away

:::

Black Picket Fence

She came in the wake of my destruction
From nothing
I paved a way of pain for her to rust in
And she trusted

The same old things I claimed
Were found corrupted
Ending up in the range
a brain would take to feel or function like a compass

A way out, means stay out
Every path that's new to the same house
We can hang hope and even blame doubt
But I know exit signs, and all the escape routes

She's not running from me
Not after she said she'd stay down
So, I lock a door here, and toss a key there
Now we're locking eyes, we nod; and we bear

With nowhere else to turn
We each come to terms
With the burn and the churn
In the hopes of what's to learn

This hallway's a crawl space
I've been here and content
Every tear is a trench
'til commandeered through the vents

Top tier dramatics
From the basement to the attic
Love looms in the living room
And her face is a fireplace

But every flame looked the same
I gazed for days and stayed
By the windowpane of stains and scars
Now the bedrooms a tomb made of gloom

Only safe that I'd assume
That the back and front lawn are for dawn
And fencing in feelings foregone
As these walls break out in song

They talk and sing of what seldom lacks
Of the secrets left swept 'neath the welcome mat
All of the topics in the closets
And not a dry space in the driveway

:::

Counting Clouds

All of my friends, lovers with potential
Past and present chaperones
Of the Shangri-La
Shape shifted into shock value
Leaving meaningful results of damage
Behind, for the future we'd never find

Living is harder than loving
At least loving lets you know
Heartbreak is coming

Unconditionally
Indiscriminately
Relentlessly
Ripping at the seams of a daydream

Pulling at what's thought
Forgetting all that's taught
Missing what's not caught
Clinging to what's clean
Submerged in the dirt of what seems

But living
O' but living
To be grateful of the guile
At the top of a pile
All the while wearing a smile

In shattered shoes for a mile
Trekking through some trials
Down razor-lined aisles
Just to end on an isle
Counting clouds
Concluding what's vile
Hurt hides from who spies.

Just outside of a mountainous hind
Those shattered shoes are but whose?
Now worn ‘til they're torn
To the top of tranquility
In an effort to view what riles

Because peace
O' said peace
Needs a release and a wrench from reality

Where friends and falsehoods frolic
And lovers leave traces of trust
And daydreams die down within dust
But discoveries happen in doubt
Where the mind finds an easy way out

Saddened on a summit
Forth and found coming
‘til tracked to the top of what traps
Floor bound is your face
Unbalanced and bottomed

They say 6 feet
But you should be damned
If you think
Or believe it's only that deep

Surely there's a core
Latched to light and what's in store
I woke when hours were wee
Begging for more
In dire need to see the day
Knowing newness was near
And enough is never had.

Until I'm gone
Like a gust when it thrusts by breaths
Never minding the last or the rest
We're only at our best when put to a test

And no one ever failed
They only grew pale
When they forgot to breathe
Holding tongues with their teeth
Like the Sun didn't seep
To a Moon and a maiming by midnight
Friends, and potential lovers
On stage in front of stars
Synchronized and scarred

Alive & alarmed
Fine and unharmed
With yesterday in our arms

All & all
Thick & thin
Nevermore
Nonetheless
Take a breath
Feel me out

:::

Wilted Lilies

If for no more than but once
I'd much rather feel clean
To heed an apology
To cry; at the sight of anything dead

I picked wilted lilies
Held them safe 'til they were black
Reminiscent of holding a hand
That never held back

With such certainty of this circumstance
I'm now filthy, rich with vitriol / automatic;
and apathetic / unclean / unclear
Couldn't care less / cackling in a cave
Contemplating some, coup de grâce

So call it crazy; tell me lies
Don't go spoiling my surprise
I can hold onto forever
With the right amount of time

O', but time / time is but a whore
A ticking tease / circling in a dance
Giving nothing but less of itself
Using nothing but hands
Stroking and striking me clockwise

I made a home from what hurts
Through each gift in what's cursed
Running in the rain

Dragging lilies from the dirt
Unfaithful to my faculty
I never knew I'd be lethal
To kill you in front of these people
How's this sidewalk a Cathedral?

I picked wilted lilies
Held them safe ‘til they were black
Reminiscent of holding your hand
Though you never held back

Now goosebumps act as seeds
A conjured-up catalyst
To help my body plant itself
here / down / way down / further

These eyes are like cursors
Planted and perjured for nervure now
Blasé & bound to what tightens
Too bright to be blinded

The height of the night makes a mark
Stars are the scars that the sky couldn't hide
Pulsing upon me in the park
With my fists full of lilies
just as dark as the day we let go

:::

Riverside Relics

There's a level of suspension
It requires all that is still
You can feel it by the water
If you close your eyes in calm

A river once showed me
Not a ripple was lonely
With my arms to their extent
I slapped space in its face

Once upon an eyelid
Imagination came to strike
No such thing was better
Than the water in my eyes

Contemplations never felt so customary
Killing time with no more than a caution
To hear the rush of the river
While my face was all wet

But then it started raining
As if the sky wanted to hide
I let it all fall on my face
Until no one could tell
The difference between
raindrops & tears

⁝⁝⁝

O.D.

It wasn't the first time
The sidewalks lit up with light
Succumbing to the breaking of bright
You were soaking up the silver in the sequence

The city sleeps on its side
The rations of good faith fall short
Crooked street signs donated shade
The needle in your broken record played

Track marks and footprints in your veins
Your eyes displayed the daze
We've both seen better days
I wish you were high enough to pray

A one-way road offered you a bed
The only thing left in that pine box
is dead
Your procession gave us all high beams to swallow

And I'm in the car behind your hearse
Wishing I was first

:::

Your Smile Against My Frown

Your smile against my frown
Enlightenment through my doubt
Enticing, but intense; like violence in a crowd
I was styling in my shroud
All the while weighed down
By trials that piled atop my crown

Pride was protruding
Preventing what's proven to provide
The faith in which some leap of
You seek, every dead-end I don't speak of
Stretched to the rest of the edge
Pleading to be plucked from a pledge
Like a promise protected by prelude(s)

No need to worry
Though your face is buried
Know, that I'm only in a hurry
to heal; everything that's already hurting
Like thin skin gripped by a touch that twists
Now turning
Bent
Bruised
Blessed
by the bond of what's burning
Between

I held your hair at the helm
As you hurled out the unreachable
Transitioning what's teachable
Throwing up all you in thrall
Staining
Like painting
On the walls I built
Tall
Crashing to the call
Dropping to the drips you drooled
Demolishing the dread in a dream

A regurgitated reality
Rectified in a disguise I recognized
Like I looked into your eyes
And managed to make out a mirror
Reflecting my wrongs
Right in your retinas
Cramped by clouds
In your pupils' background
For the sake of what's seen
For crying out loud

I long to be strong
Strung along and strapped to be plowed
Through the noise that is near and announced
Deafened, by the sound you once found
Side by side we lie
With our ears against the Earth
Grinning on the ground

L-O-V-E...

Four Letters That Hurt

UNKNOWN THE POET

ABOUT THE AUTHOR

Unknown the Poet [aka Wade Staark] is a man that loves to express himself through art. Based out of Los Angeles, California, his works are a result of his own experiences and emotions, fueled further by inspiration from the world around him. He writes with the hope that his words will reach as many hearts as possible, impacting the lives of his readers in a positive manner. Readers, who have since become friends. Unknown the Poet joined the Magesoul Publishing team as a Home Author in 2019 and with two books already released, "Life Isn't Perfect, Neither Is This Book" and "Piece by Piece", this author is well on his way to achieving his goals. To find out more, please visit www.unknownthepoet.com where you can also purchase his books and merchandise.

Connect with him on social media:

 @unknownthepoet

:::

I'm Not Stupid, Just In Love

I knew what you were up to.
The same footprints
that stomped on my heart.
Were the same ones
walking right
through
his front door.

⁝⁝⁝

Linen Secrets

We've done this before.
Late night meets,
Trying to fill voids casted
By ex-lovers.
For these few hours
We forget about it all,
Only to remember when the sun rises.
You sleep,
I stay awake,
Knowing I'm still as empty
As when we started.
You sleep yet
Your moans haunt
The silence of this
Hotel room.

:::

What's Seen Can't Be Unseen

I forgive,
but I never forget.
For the image of what you did
is forever branded,
in fire and blood,
on the back of my eyelids.

⁝⁝⁝

Lifeless Wounds

I showed her my battle wounds.
Wounds from all my past heartbreaks,
she said she would help heal me,
instead she feasted on my weakness.
Love, loves!
But love also hurts!
And when it hurts,
it leaves no trace of life.

⁝⁝⁝

Unapologetic gift

I give—
Only to be taken and discarded.
She said she was different,
She said she cared.
Late night sexting and
Good morning messages;
I told her I was scared to fall in love,
She said to not fear and
To just let things happen.
It was too late—
I gave in, to her manipulative ways and
Fell harder than the sun sets.
After all we went through,
She selfishly put a bow on herself,
And gave her heart
To someone else.

:::

Ulterior Motives

He said that he hated
to see her cry,
Meanwhile,
as she lay sobbing on the floor,
Black eyes,
bloody lips,
his pants,
told a different story.

⁝⁝⁝

1 Cup of Pain

We really wrote the recipe
For heartbreak, didn't we?
½ a cup of You,
½ a cup of Me,
2 tablespoons of the past,
3 pinches of lies and
1 gallon of fucking!
How does one measure a broken soul?
Just throw that shit in too.
Cook on high, until burnt and undesirable.
Pain is suffered in degrees;
That can’t be gauged.

⁝⁝⁝

Beep, Beep, Beep

I can't sleep, the time ticks away
with every toss and turn
I lose another second,
than a minute,
Now an hour.
My mind is overloaded
With broken pieces of heart and soul,
No room for sleep.
Once I close my eyes,
My fucking alarm beeps.
Beep!
I can't sleep!
Beep!
I can't sleep!
Beep!
I can't sleep!
Insomnia has me beat.

⁝⁝⁝

Note to Self

I feel worthy of love,
Because my friends and family,
Tell me I deserve it.
I feel I am not always the problem,
Because my therapist told me so.
I feel I can forget and numb this urge
To delete myself permanently,
Because my pills help allow me to.
Even with all of this,
Through the years—
I have finally come to accept,
Something on my own.
No friends or family,
No therapist,
No pills…
I have come to accept,
This lifetime was just not
The one I was destined to shine in.
Better luck next time.

:::

Hollow

No matter how you look at it,
Hurt is required.
How else will you know,
What true happiness feels like?
All happiness and no pain,
Is a tragic canvas painted with lies.
Would you rather
Never have known what could have been?
Not knowing sometimes is worse than the pain.
We need the sad and heavy—
To balance the emptiness of the unknown.

⁝⁝⁝

Do I Even Exist?

I haven't felt like myself in a while
I tend to get lost in the thought
of where I could have lost "Me".
It's hard to gauge really.
How does one measure the distance,
between here and nowhere?
In my opinion it's impossible
to retrace those steps,
just to reclaim a part of me
I probably won't even recognize.
chuckle
Sadness.
Loneliness.
This corner.
This is me now,
and it's between here
and nowhere.

:::

I Miss You

I miss receiving
Your random, silly photos.
I miss the
“Good Morning”
“I’m thinking about you”
“Good Night”
Text messages.
I miss the video chats.
I miss the feeling of missing you.
You didn’t have to be there
To make me feel special,
Just the idea
Of you existing somewhere,
Reciprocating my feelings,
Was strong enough
To make me fall in love with you.
I miss you.

My Soul Didn t Break, It Saved Me

SOSHINIE SINGH

ABOUT THE AUTHOR

Editor Soshinie Singh, is a Guyanese author, poet and twin flames guide. She is very enthusiastic, and her energy is contagious. She aims to spread unconditional love and empowering messages to the young, as well as to the old. Soshinie believes that no matter what stage of life someone is in, it is never too late to gain clarity about recent or past problems. This is what she provides through her gentle nature, as well as upliftment to people's everyday lives. Her words come from a sacred place, and from her experiences which she uses to touch the lives of others, as well as to motivate them. Soshinie is someone many would describe as an old soul, and she is wise beyond her years. She is also on the path of awakening her gifts so she can share it with the rest of the world and live abundantly. Her books, The Phoenix Letters and The Phoenix Letters Return can be purchased at Amazon and The Book Depository.

Connect with Soshinie on social media:

 @soshiniesingh.author

 www.lifewithyoualways.com/

:::

Shine Like Gold

I look into the eyes of endurance;
with a fierceness I feel in my skin.
And I blow thoughts of dandelions
as mere superstitions
that all will shine like gold one day.
- I hope, not everything I wish for
would elude me...

⁝⁝⁝

Return

I request -
Bring the light back
into your eyes,
they are calling for closure
and a little friendliness to last.
I am proud of what we created
I am proud of what we have shown each other
and though it's time to go separate ways
I know you'll be okay.
Until we meet again...
...someday...

:::

Fall Short

Where did I fall short?
Maybe, I did not love you enough
because I didn't make it
to the beginning of your day.
Maybe, I've just placed myself in a heart,
that couldn't love me,
the same.

⁝⁝⁝

Scattered Pieces

Where did the pieces of me go scattered?
I am still looking for the girl I can love.
Maybe, after all the faking
I have not reached that point yet,
where my skin would stop crawling
from all the mistakes—
I've committed.

:::

Dreams

For quite some time,
I'd forgotten what it was like to dream,
basking in those nights where
sleep would evade me,
or a blank canvas would be waiting for me
to paint something;
until, those nightly illusions commenced
their onslaught of craziness once again,
showing me the things,
I mostly wanted cornered by those I feared.
- And what I hated most of all about them,
were the scars they implanted on my body
like tracking devices.
Finding me wherever I went,
consuming my thoughts,
even though I knew,
they were just dreams,
sometimes, they had a tendency
of leaving me shattered,
irrespective
of what's real.

:::

The Curse of Insecurities

My insecurities,
they come like nightmares
which paralyze me
and keep me pinned for hours at a time,
and sometimes,
they are hard to break out of,
because being lost in your head
is a journey requiring a road map.
So, my insecurities appear
like nightmares,
rendering me lost
until I find the light again,
the light which would lead me to believe,
in the power,
of my heart.

::::

Without effort

I'll try to get out of bed,
and maybe paint a smile.
to welcome today,
as the bright sunny day,
it lends itself to be.
And hopefully I'll learn
to wear the glow
with not much effort-
one day.

⁝⁝⁝

Splinter

There is a splinter,
embedded deep in my heart,
protruding like a spike.
But I cannot seem to pry it loose,
else it threatens,
for my heart to bleed out.

⁝⁝⁝

Finding Me

I didn't find myself
when my heart was whole,
I found me
when it was coming apart
each perfect seam at a time.
As it drowned me,
in a nightmare of threads,
merging and converging,
I stared into the
stringy eyes of emptiness,
to see a destiny
weaving my path,
intricately.

.

⁝⁝⁝

Chasing Shadows

I am chasing shadows
of my imagination,
courting those dreams
that would one day abandon me,
and make tears into my home.

- I regretted that thing I wished for.

⁝⁝⁝

Letdown

"You are a letdown"

"I am a letdown"

Ugly words that I have
uttered to myself.
Thought,
felt,
and in the end,
those words have been causing a riot,
throwing stones against my own heart,
shattering pulses for glass,
until, I cut and bleed to see-

I am not a letdown.

Just someone learning through
the moments that let me down.
- I am not those moments,
I am, how I evolve, from those moments.

⁝⁝⁝

Vacant Land

I get ready to take a dive
into my heart,
but from the heights
overlooking my depths,
I notice how truly
empty my land has become.
I wait for new seeds to bloom,
after they have plowed me thoroughly,
and robbed me of all I could have been.

Love Can Never Hurt

PARTH

ABOUT THE AUTHOR

Born in India, Parth discovered a love to express himself through words at the age of fourteen and has been writing thirteen years now. He believes that love is never the reason for someone's pain, the lack of it is and it is this pain, that may take you to a dark place, but can also show you the light. It is because of his belief that pain is beautiful, that he uses the pen name "Beautifully Painful".

"Pain forces you to grow and to see love as the true beauty it is - one which forges a connection with two people. To have sometimes, nothing but memories left over one day."

Connect with Parth on social media:

 @beautifully_painful

:::

Open the door.
I have come to see your heart,
its history, galore
I want to capture, your art.
Your hands, made by accident
your eyes designed for treason
but they made a permanent dent
and you stayed faithful
for my reasons.
So, open the door.
I have come to watch you laugh
in these days of unfaithful passion.
I have come to live, in your aggression.
Let the winds ponder for your scent
and the flowers die in your wait.
I will hold you tight,
'til I descend
such is your power,
your strength.

⁝⁝⁝

The curtains dropped,
the show had stopped,
life was real again.
Before I could even say a word,
she'd left,
my voice left unheard,
this, the greatest theft.
How could I live?
I'd lost my rhymes,
in this betrayal by time
But soon after I closed my eyes,
I saw hers watching mine.
But for her lovers' smile,
she could cry a mile.
And within those beautiful tears,
she hid her deepest fears.
So I gave my heart to her, to lease.
Finally, her soul, at peace.
And mine, at least…
can breathe—

For now.

:::

This wait is a raging fire
that can burn down stars,
like how our hearts burn
through the distance.
The world has left us in pain
and unintended scars.
Bring me to your light
there is so much to die for,
in the moment of bliss,
I ignored the love I cry for;
yet the heart takes no hits and
becomes more to live for.
I watch you
from the eyes of my soul
and wonder,
there are thousands of poets
that write you as their muse,
I urge them to forget having you.
Even in their rhymes,
they can use their blood to write,
it would be of no use.
I was tied to your energy
because I am yours,
yet some question,
the credibility of my worth.
My nights shine to keep me awake
so I can work to open doors,

to the home we love,
to the home I dream,
in which we make love.
Bring to me your dark,
there is so much to adore.
Such is the beauty,
anything that touches you,
becomes pure.
I am the music that plays in the rain,
not the blues,
They think I am diseased,
but can't see, that you're my cure.
I am walking and running,
flying to let you know,
through the storms in the ocean,
I am ready to row,
for a love this deep
puts the oceans to shame,
the moon has no right but to
sing for our fame.
I question no one,
I love only you.
Kept apart not by honour itself,
but the honour of a love that is true.
Planets are stars
if looked upon with your eyes,
you love me not?
Don't live eternally,
in these lies.

Bring me your soul
and your hell,
they belong to me.
I will come to them
if they can't come to see,
that I have built a world
that resides in the entirety
of soul,
without you, without me,
these poems are never whole.
We let the stars live
for they want us more,
our beds stained with shame
without our love on their floor.
I know the day I return,
there'll be no lock on that door.
The day we return,
there will be pain,
no more.

⁝⁝⁝

I only hope that when
you think of love,
you'll think of me.

That when it rains,
you'll think of me.

⁝⁝⁝

I stood at the top of the mountains,
looking down at the houses built with bricks,
and watched memories untold on trains,
with clouds and rains playing tricks.

With the delicate souls tangled in music,
the roads led to pain and joy,
they travelled with the most peaceful acoustic,
as children played with sticks as toys.

There is life in these hills,
which the greatest don't see,
it has stories of magic and honest thrills,
from which our cities flee.

Let's dance under the rains and the stars,
make wild chases of the moon,
and treasure our childhood scars.
For if life were to end in this cities dust,
we would already be dead,
for this unwanted lust.

::::

Since we met
I have not known nights
where I do not scream,
for your arms.

:::

Today we hoped for tomorrow
to keep us closer
without a need to borrow time.
But time was our enemy
with the impending departure
we knew we had to live for this last memory.
It was like yesterday, that we first met
and time just rolled.
Now she's buried her face in my shirt,
holding my hand and my soul.
The minute I held her close she cried,
tears dripping like blood, from a rose.
All flirtatiousness dissolved,
as kisses slowed and tears flowed.
What a favour, to have breathed together,
one that could be seen reflected in her eyes.
Our words did not match what we felt,
yet sacrifice was not, our way of life.
How could I say goodbye
to the sun or, the night?
For even the rains cry
when the sun and moon fight.
We left together,
out of love for each other,
but as I look at my wall of fame,
our memories reveal in pictures,
a still-burning, flame.

:::

As I walked down my path,
I was lost,
even with the address on my palm.
I found houses of smiles and laughs,
but hidden pains,
sounded alarms.

I don’t wake early these days,
since asked
if I’m a coward, who ignores truth’s face.
I hide from the sun and its rays,
since asked,
if too lazy, to win the race.

I unheard their questions,
remained oblivious
to their gaze.
Kept walking to find
where my home was,
as their hate echoed through my days.

When the place I’d been
searching for,
came into sight
I hesitated, confused,
used to pain
and lonely nights.

I didn't know how to accept
a home,
inviting, full of love.
When the only one I'd known,
was devoid of light,
damp and dark

So I walked,
further alone,
Except for her scent,
that clung to
and followed me
round every bend.

This earth so jealous of her love,
would steal it,
if it could,
So I keep walking,
holding on, perhaps
a little tighter than I should.

I can't lose her to this world,
can't let her out
of my sight.
She is everything that keeps me
on a path of what's
true and right.

So let me walk
'til she's gone,
until she decides to leave.
For in this war I fight
I've spent
enough time on my knees.

And if that day should come,
it will be with my last breath.
For the only thing that can
come between us,
is the one they call, 'Death"

:::

We sat at the edge
of the illusion of eternity.
Knowing it was a weak ledge,
in this cruel world.
In silence,
I wept in her arms,
as she, melted in my tears
unaware of her power.
We danced together
amidst monsoon showers.
But as I gained a clear head
I realised I'd been led
into the arms of hell;
because she was leaving,
without opportunity to
complete our tale.
It was not her choice to leave
but our fate was always destined
to be one of grief.
Patiently I wait
for the rains to come again.
For summer's heat to pass
and winter's showers to return.
Patiently I wait
to repeat this seasonal blunder.
She. My favourite season.
We. Condemned,
to be torn asunder.

::::

How can I let go,
when the fire of our relationship
is felt even in the ashes
of love that remain?

(Can't)

Finding My Voice

BROOKE STORY

ABOUT THE AUTHOR

Coming from a family of artists, Brooke Story has a deep-rooted love and appreciation for all forms of creative expression. A California native, and mother of two, Brooke has always utilized writing to purge and process her thoughts and feelings. She rediscovered her love of poetry while battling post-partum depression and suffering through a miscarriage when she stumbled across the poetry and writing communities on Instagram. Her writing style is non-conforming and transparent; each piece is unique unto itself, varying in topic, and hits readers with an outpouring of her most intimate and intricate vulnerabilities. Brooke's love for words and wordplay shows through her work as she often takes readers on a journey of unexpected structure and unpattern rhyme, with hints of alliteration sprinkled throughout.

"I have made so many meaningful connections through reading and writing that I will forever hold dear to my heart. A huge thank you to my family and friends, and to readers everywhere. A special thank you to my parents and children, who have seen me at my worst but still loved me the best, and to those who have extended their hand to me. I love you all." -Brooke Story

Connect with Brooke on social media:

 @thepoetbiz

:::

Pendulum Heart

He built the wooden porch
she had always envisioned
would elevate their modest shanty.

One honey-dripped morning,
he clasped his affections
inside a golden heart-shaped locket
and slipped it over her head.

Onlookers flocked
as she stood proudly on her new deck,
boasting her flashy necklace for all to see...
not realizing it was a noose.

But the crowd knew,
and only felt slightly guilty
as they swayed along
to the creaking metronome
as she swung from the gallows.

⁝⁝⁝

1, 2, 3

At first it was my life- myself, just for me
Then one day by chance, along came he
Oh, he made my heart smile
And so after awhile
He asked for my hand in matrimony.

Together we planned a path, you see
A smart one including a Master's Degree
That he had wanted to get
Since before we had met
But, whoops, us two became us three.

That changed our course, naturally
Since we now had a new responsibility
Sure, some things were shelved
But we were beside ourselves
In love with this tiny new entity.

We did our best, wholeheartedly
And in truth, in all complete honesty
Things between us went bad
But we held tightly to what we had
Until it grew into me, now plus three.

Then something changed, most drastically
I broke, somehow, after that last delivery
I guess it's not rare
For women who bear
Children grown inside their own wombs, sadly.

So, we (and by that, I mean he and me)
Tried hard to save us, most desperately
But the hem had unraveled
Through those years we had traveled
Having already fallen apart at the seams.

One last surprise, for both he and me
That our two were now going to become our three
There were mixed emotions
But we shared family devotion
Until that last little addition never came to be.

That last thread had broken, finally
The one holding together our small family
Though we had fought for so long
For our bond to stay strong
We still fell apart at the end, quite rapidly.

And now, it's back to he and me
Our union dissolved, a new kind of "we"
With time now to reflect
Hard truths in retrospect
That some things in life aren't meant be.

I bleed the ink to pen my journeys
Expose myself in the lines for all eyes to see
I take all of life's hits
And flip the script on that shit
Seeking the beauty that lies in life's miseries.

:::

Shellshock

As I lie in silence,
surrendered to your forces,
I'm lost in the breathtaking beauty
of snow falling delicately around me,
blanketing my body.
O, to catch just one snowflake
upon my tongue!
Eyes closed,
mouth opened,
tongue outstretched.

Drifting...

back to times where we lay next to each other
in much the same way-
spent and euphoric.
Floating
after succumbing to ecstasy.
Skin as sheets, awash in sweat.
Panting
broken by gentle flutters of giddy laughter.
Stealing glances at each other
from under the soothing hum
of a ceiling fan.
It's soft cool breeze
sweeping up after us
as we are lulled to sleep.

But here,
now,
I'm fighting to see.
Shivering uncontrollably
though not cold.
Nose and throat burning
as I reach for the assuredness
of your hand,
only to grab a fistful of white powder.

You are not here.
I am not upon our fiery bed of passion.

Alas,
this is our battlefield.
And, I'm laid to rest
under the raining ash
of you.

Just

one

last

taste.

Laughter at a Funeral

Restless,
in these retched recesses
of self-reflection.
It reeks in here
of resentful sentiments.
Perhaps it's my penchant
for reckless weekends;
the tension in my weakness
for collecting remnants
that bear some semblance
to my heart's past tenants.

Maybe that's what sealed my sentence.

My penance,
to be enclosed and entombed
forced to lick old wounds.
I'm getting so claustrophobic in this room,
where there's no room to roam.
I'm trapped
in my heart's comatose catacombs,
tripping on trophies of catastrophes-

toxic taxidermy bodies
stuffed and stacked upon my shelves
alongside precarious versions of me,
various persons I used to be,
lackluster labels I used to laugh
and call myself
nonchalantly.

All I can do is pick up the pieces
of broken pick-up lines and
discarded punch-card heart diseases,
collected from past lifetimes
from broken timelines
littering this old floor
strewn about like contagious cold sores
looking for lips to lock out on a
damp and desperate dancefloor.

They're abrasions of my past revelations,
receipts of pounding heart palpitations
from those who lined up to play,
but were incapable of remaining stable.
So we flatlined,
and here now they lay
flayed and splayed
upon my display tables.

⁝⁝⁝

The Power of Words

He'd scoff,
"Who said?"

Ugh! Those two fucking words
still ringing in my ears,
locked behind two pressed lips
for two long fucking years.

For way too many years,
it appears.

"Who said?"

Don't really answer that,
it's rhetorical, see?
It means, "How dare you think
or act as if you're free."

When my actions aren't free,
apparently.

"Who said?"

A statement, not question,
when things don't go his way;
an, "I think it's funny
how you think you have a say."

An, "I think it's funny
how I hear your words voiced,
as if you have a choice."

"Who said?"

Two simple fucking words
repeated over time
serves as a reminder
"Thou shalt not undermine."
For his reign is supreme;
how dare I cross that line?
To think that anything's not his,
but instead mine.

But...
a cool thing happens when
you shift your point of view,
you realize your worth
really lies within you.
None can really dictate
what you can/cannot do-
only if and unless
you choose/allow them to.

It took me way too long
to get this simple fact into my head,
"Who said?" really DOES ask a question.

"I did.
I just fucking said."

Memories

CARLOS MEDINA

ABOUT THE AUTHOR

Carlos Medina is not only a respected author and published poet – but also the founder and CEO of Magesoul Publishing. Carlos, a Bronx New York native, is well known for sharing his talent on Instagram and Facebook. His writing began five years ago, after the end of his marriage. At this time, Carlos started traveling through the deepest crevices of his heart, mind, and soul. Through this exploration, the readers have been encouraged and invited to join him on his journey and to reflect upon their own. The insight he offers and the way he weaves his words leaves readers exploring their deeper selves in ways they never have before. Carlos's passion and outpouring of emotion have led him to publish seven successful and soulful books.
In August 2017, Carlos found another calling in helping and guiding others. This is when he created his business- Magesoul Publishing. He has enabled numerous other writers and poets to create the books they only dreamt of, guiding them each step of the way in both their writing and journey and enabling their art to reach others.

Connect with Carlos on social media:

@magesoul

@magesoul1

www.magesoul.com

@magesoul

:::

The First Day

I've tried. I've tried to live every day as a human that's experienced pain at its fullest. The damage you've caused me will be with me throughout my life.

I've tried to start again, I've tried to love again, for god sake, I've tried so hard to love myself. No one has a clue of how much I remind myself daily about this. But it's hard. It's hard to love someone again. It's hard to open up my heart them, and I feel so fucking guilty each time I look at her eyes. Because I know that deep down inside she loves me, but I'm scared. I'm terrified to let her in.

Each time I get closer to opening that door within me, I back off and begin to see all the negative things, I begin to feel that it wouldn't work out. Although I know that it will, that there is a chance that her and I will spend this lifetime united, the damage from you still has a way of crawling back out. These are my every day mental battles, these are weaknesses but I know and continue to fight through.

It hurts, but I know I will push forward each day as if it was the first day that I met her and the first moment that I actually stopped feeling emotions for who you once were to me.

:::

Mother

Today I look back and reflect on my childhood.

As I go deeper within my mind, I see you. I see a strong woman doing her best to raise her children. I see a mother that sacrificed everything for the safety of her kids.

I know I never took the opportunity to tell you, but I want you to know that I truly love you. I thank you for everything you have done. I know it wasn't easy Mom, but you did the best you could.

I know we've been through a lot together: nights going to bed without food, nights with candles being our only source of light because we couldn't afford electricity, and clothing from second-hand stores. If I had the chance to trade it all, I simply wouldn't because I got to have you always by my side.

Mom, I hope that I've made you proud of who I have become. I'm not perfect, but I try my best. With every part of my body, every chamber in my mind and every pathway in my soul. I want you to know that I will love you beyond the existence of every universe created.

I love you Mom.

:::

Father

God, what I would've done to know who you were.

You see, you neglected us when I was 6 years old. You gave in to the bottle and forgot what it meant to have a family. It's so much knowing that there is a possibility that I have a lot of similarities with you.

What I would do to be hugged by you. To smell your cologne and feel that presence I deserved from a father. But it's too late now.

You're gone. You left me without a goodbye or an apology for not being there when I needed you the most. But I forgive you. I forgive you because I know you had no clue on how to be a Dad.

Perhaps the almighty will let you take a peek into my life for a few seconds and you could see how I turned out. I'm trying my best to not be like you. But I'm told that I look just like you. They even tell me you were a writer.

God, I wish I had the chance to read your work, to sit there with you and just share everything I feel inside. I know you would probably be the only person to understand my emotions and assure me that it's ok.

Wherever you're at pop, I want you to know that I'm carrying your last name with dignity and pride. I hope you're proud of what I've become Pop. R.I.P.

Your son,

Carlos Medina

:::

Son

Here I am again, my son. Knees on the ground in front of your stone. It has been a while, my boy. You know, if you were still here, you would be 10 years old right now. I would be looking into your eyes and thanking the almighty for such a blessing.

I'm sorry things didn't turn out the way I pictured them. I know you and I didn't have control over the situation. But today son, I was walking by a park and I saw a boy with his father playing catch. I thought about you, I thought how much fun we would've had playing catch or even going to the baseball games. So many emotions ran through me that I had to take a seat on the bench and calm myself down.

I wish I had the chance to show you how to ride a bike and be the first one there to catch you each time you fell. It hurts so much, but I know you're doing good up there. I know you've become an angel to many and I hope you help them in their times of need.

Last year was hard for me, kiddo. Christmas came around and I sat there in front of our Christmas tree. I felt like you were there with me. I even placed your first present there just so you could know that you're still in my heart.

My son... you just have no idea how much I love you and miss you. Knowing that you're in a better place is what keeps me going. Keep being God's helper, my son.

Love,
Dad

:::

Daughter

My sweet little angel.

You probably won't be able to read this until like 15 years later. You see, I'm writing this to you before you're actually born.

I want you to know that I've been waiting for your arrival for a long time. You see, I know you're going to be a precious angel sent from heaven. You will be a blessing to me and your mother. Without knowing, you will be the one to help us sail this marriage into the future.

I can't wait to finally hold you in my arms and tell everyone, this is my beautiful daughter. I want you to know that I will be forever by your side. Unlike my father, you will have a father to be with you every step of the way. I'll be there for you when you take your first step and on your first day of school. You see, it has been my desire for a long time to wake up every day and see that beautiful face of who I would call my child.

When the moment comes that you feel sick, I'll be there for you my little angel. The time will come when you will become a young woman, god knows how I fear that most. I know you will fall in love, and someone will come and hurt your feelings, I'll be there for you and you can cry away on my chest.

What I want you to know my little angel is: you will not have to face anything in this world alone. You will have your mother and myself there for you. You, my little angel, are not alone. That is my promise to you.

That is our promise to you.

⁝⁝⁝

Eulogized

I'm scared. I'm in a place that I never thought I would be in. Standing here, right in front of your casket, holding your hand and beginning to visualize how your life was lived. I'm seeing it all in glimpses and I can't control the amount of emotions that I'm feeling. The moment you began to crawl, to the moment you started school, the days that you cried in class because you feared being alone. I remember it clearly how you called upon your Mom. I never heard you ever complain about her, I guess she was your heart from the time of your birth.

Your hands are so cold now, you always had these warm hands, just like your heart. You always seemed to warm any person that crossed your path with troubles. I remember the time that you fell in love for the first time. God how happy you were. But that didn't last long like many things in your life.

The only thing that ever lasted were your jobs. You had this thing for work. Always a workaholic. I remember that moment that you went against all your friends and family and got married. My God, only if you would've listened to them. You would've saved yourself so many problems and heartache. But let's be honest, if she didn't divorce you, would you be the person you became? I don't think so. But damn, you really went through hell after her departure.

I'm seeing it all now, I can feel all that pain, you really did give it your all. I'm glad you forgave her, but I'm prouder that you forgave yourself. Because it really did take a tremendous toll on you.

I'm surprised by the number of people that are here today. Who would've thought you would have touched so many of them? I guess that was your gift, I guess you really did find yourself after all of this.

Hey, they even dressed you in your favorite suit. Your hair is combed to the back as you always liked it. So many roses here just as you wished. You've accomplished so many things in this world and you're leaving behind pieces of yourself for everyone.

Now I can see it all. I was actually you in this mortal world. I am your rebirth. I am the sum of all your years taken away by your death. I am you, in between the ravens and the gravestones, in between the light and its moon and in between every blink of eyes, I am YOU in what they call, the afterlife.

A Day in The Life

JACOB MARLEY

ABOUT THE AUTHOR

Jacob Marley is one of the newest members of the Magesoul Publishing Family and is set to contribute to all three books in the new Anthology Trilogy. As a writer, Jacob endeavors to captivate, intrigue, question and entertain. Coming Spring 2020 is his debut collection of works, "The Ouroboros", comprising of poetry and prose, short stories and fantasy including 100 pieces crafted in between the dark and the light.

"The words we use may be our greatest allies or most terrible weapon. Let them be the former and we will know the greatest parts of our world. I would like to thank you for reading, always."

Connect with Jacob on social media:

 @jacobmarleypress

:::

6 A.M.
[Good Morning]

This day began as the last ended,
with subsurface rumblings of discontentment.
Plans with no commencement, unconquered hills
and kite strings forgotten with a propensity for endless
possibility,
but,

No breeze to lift them...

It is this then
which has become the daily perspective,
a "good morning death wish"
and I cannot imagine a different direction
in which I found the least of intention,

For a course shift…

I need a best friend with a forklift
to raise me up above the gut
of this distended rut
of contemptment that contends with
a stuck clutch because,

I can't change gear…

And I fear this death knell alarm clock
that mocks me each pallid sunrise.
The colors have run dry long ago,
but I find some reason to continue
because the show,

Must go on…

So, I raise my wooden arms
and resemble a grandfather timepiece
that has seen midnight and noon too frequently
and has so tired of the bipolar gloom and its frequency
but,

Still right twice a day though…

And my window stares down to four flights below.
I wonder often if the fall would kill me,
or just leave me with no movement or feeling
in my arms and legs,
but,

That might be the best thing….

Because I'm so often stressing
the point of a life with no flavor to savor
no oil and vinegar no dressing just anger
and so much second guessing my craving to live…

Just one more day…

Impressed with the way
I managed to rotate
my body from out of this bed.
The sunlight streams in from the cracks
in my dead black out blinds
and my soul screams "just die!"
but my mouth shapes the words,

No, I'm fine...

No really…

I'm perfectly fine.

⁝⁝⁝

7 A.M.
[Repeat]

Motivation decapitated, emotional paralysis;
with motions conducted
and established by unanimous vote.
My congress of thought
cannot seem to cross this proverbial moat.

So stands idle instead...

I remain dripping at the river's edge
while halfheartedly cooking eggs
and selfishly imagining I am
the unborn chickens within.

Slowly burning in the pan...

Never had the famous chance
the morning's supposed to give.
Partner to a vacant dance,
I am the empty shell therein.

Not at all surprising...

The temperature is rising,
transforming my sins
into a tasty new scramble.
Must be that time to begin.

My shambling existence...

My orchestra conducts
symphonic resistance to the monotone
but it's less than little assistance,
to defeating the horrors shown
on cyclical loop of persistence.

For on it drones...

While I burn my toast.
Like this day and the one before,
its refrain is beyond reproach;
because I deserve nothing more.

Not even these eggs.

:::

8 A.M.
[Traffic]

I feel like I'm crawling into my own coffin.
Four wheels and steel barriers only move
me closer toward monotony.
My own death mocking me.

Ha. Ha. Ha.

Over enthusiastic voices claw at my ears
begging my acquiescence to a society
that values only the blood of my wallet...
a worthless name on paper with a credit score.

Money. Money. Money.

I raise hollow prayers to be more.
No one is listening. It’s sickening.
Yet I keep driving on toward a treadmill
on which to pretend that I am thriving.

Run. Run. Run.

Surviving is a rich man's game.
I never learned the rules or how to play.
I just make motions of humanity
as I walk through the doors.

In. Out. In.

Fake smiles shine, hands wave
While empty pleasantries steal my words.
My reflection is one I don't recognize.
Work to work to work to die.

Lie. Submit. Lie.

Fulfillment is a lovely dream. A fantasy.
A fallacy. An echo of things that won't ever be.
The carrot dancing at the end of a string.
Yet, I am the marionette.

Step. Step. Step.

A man defined by a suit and tie wanders by
And suggests I smile more.
"Any day above ground is a good one!"
So sayeth him to the whore.

Click. Click. Click.
Check a box.

Monday... Tuesday...

Tick. Tick. Tick.
Check a clock.

Wednesday... Thursday...

Sick. Sick. Sick.
Fucking stop.

T.G.I.F.

:::

10 A.M.
[Grind]

In the dimly lit corridors behind my vision,
views of my own transgressions are
obscured.
Caustic lessons hard earned decorate the walls,
simply gathering dust.

What is learned is misremembered, though
I must run my fingers over the scars in the
halls more often than not
because I feel their depressions even when
absent the touch.

These days now though seem much the same.
Replay. Replay. Replay.
Slow motion highlights. What a shame,
you've missed another social call.
It all appears a blur.

Pronoun, adjective, verb...they quietly wait.
Desperate to slake a thirst that can never
be quenched.
Drenched in the machinations
of a malevolent mind.

Time to draft your reports:
Endless monotonous drone? Check.
Always feeling alone? Check.
A question of things unknown? Check.
Is my sanity slipping? Check.

Faucets raucously dripping? Check.
Mental Chinese water torture?
Check. Check. Check.
Do it all for the rent.
Clock out. Relent.

Check... Check... Check.

How do you undress a moment?
See it naked in the daylight lonesome,
hoping for clarity...
Another embarrassing thought...
I am not who they think I am.

Son of Sam synaptic response.
I see a dog outside.
He makes me laugh.
Oh wait...it's reflective glass.
Or maybe it’s not.

I think I'd rather not ask.

:::

12 P.M.
[Lunch Date]

Its lunch time, but I don’t want to eat.

I sit alone on a bench inhaling the toxic
reprieve of my first cigarette in hours.
My coworkers are guzzling gossip
and the day's latest trendy latte.
I can barely choke down the scene.
It's appalling to me,
the epitome of degradation.

There's no salvation in their forced laughter.

Just, water cooler banter,
which remains corpse-like in its animation
behind their mouths.
Living tongues speaking undead language.
Voodoo doll zombies
pin pricked into motion.

Devotion to the devil’s trade.

Rolling emotions play like a PowerPoint
presentation across their faces
dulled light projected from their eyes
and still envy rides its verdant horse
through my veins causing my blood to boil.

I could never be so simply joyous.

Even my daily improv show lacks such
luster and laughter.
Empty throats only howl with abandon
when the stage lights dim.
I am in no such position to argue with them,
though,

They are mostly right.

I'm undeserving of their applause.
The sound of one hand clapping seems
my entire existence.
A persistent slapping of the air,
connections lacking.

They probably all have a group chat.

⁞⁞⁞

2 P.M.
[Doubt]

I am the vacancy of permanence.
Your internal acquiescence.
Care not for words I've ever sent,
I probably never meant it.

The graveyard shift of second guessing.
A mortuary house of cards.
Praising sin that turns from blessing,
a hymnal sung by muted bards.

I am the swaying flowers frozen stiff.
The petals lacking luster.
The ice compelling their paralysis.
the hole in which you are torn asunder.

Your thoughts become irreparable.
Separate your church and state.
Your efforts once remarkable,
are left broken in my wake.

The cavernous space that occupies.
Enamored by fates of dissolution.
The mistake that tragic, multiplies.
The invalidation of resolution.

Do you feel fatigue now weigh your bones?
Coercing your defeat?
Can you hear the sad and silent moans,
begging your release?

This quiet speech alarms you see,
deliver me your questions.
Your ship is rocking violently.
Surrender to inspection.

I am your god...
Did I forget to mention?
I exist within all things
I have never known discretion.

Crown me Doubt.
I am your king.

⁝⁝⁝

6 P.M.
[Recipe for Disaster]

Cuban Picadillo

• 3 Tbsp olive oil
Needed to lubricate a jaw far too stiff.

• 1 small onion, diced
Try not to cry as you encounter it.

• ½ green bell pepper, diced
Be careful not to cut your wrist.

• 2 cloves fresh garlic, pressed or chopped well
Press them into your palms to confirm
you are not vampiric.

• 1 ½ lbs. ground beef (or vegetarian substitute)
Imagining you are cattle fit only for slaughter.

• 1 tsp. salt (or to taste)
Best throw some over your shoulder, too.

• 1 can (8 oz) chopped tomato
The fragile flesh, bloody red, sweet when then
exposed.

• 2 Tbsp. of tomato paste
Resist the urge to use as war paint
as your demons assemble.

• 1 cup dry white wine (the cheaper, the better!)
Drink the bottle, fuck the sauce.
Rinse and repeat until sauced yourself.

• 4 Tbsp. pimiento-stuffed green olives drained
(or a little more if you'd like)
The little black fruits seem like so many pupils,
carved out and staring back at me. Judging.

• 1 small box of dark raisins
(like the ones the kids put in their lunchboxes)
Raisins...the shriveled husks of long dead grapes...
how intensely relatable.

• 1 tsp. cumin
Cuneiform, hieroglyphs, Druidic runes,
all seem easier to read than my own fate.

1) Heat the olive oil in a large skillet over medium heat. Sauté the onion, green pepper and garlic until the onion is translucent.
Translucent, what an apt description of the very
person attempting to deliver such results to an onion.
I don't even like onion.

2) Add the ground beef and brown over medium heat.
***Slowly sear the flesh of the creature you intend to digest. Perhaps the vegans are right... I am indeed a monster*.**

3) Add the tomatoes, wine and tomato paste (in that order so that paste has juice to dissolve in) and continue cooking until meat is tender and completely cooked through. About 25 minutes. Add the olives and raisins and cook for another 5 minutes.
***Fuck. The wine. No more wine. Plenty of vodka though. That's a thing, right? Vodka sauce? Yes. Definitely. Time to make a cocktail then*.**

4) Serve over white rice
I didn't make any god damn rice...

5) Enjoy with friends and family!
***Consume me*.**

⁝⁝⁝

7 P.M.
[Primetime]

The nightly news is on...
it's a list of slaughter in alphabetical order,
and something is horribly wrong.

Zenith approaches, blazing colors dance
effervescent. Frantic, gigantic heights
intensify, juxtaposing kitten like
miniatures. Nevertheless, opposition
positions queens; relentlessly savoring
terribly unusual vehemence.
Welcoming Xerxes' young.

Appalling! Yesterday's born colorless due
each familiarity. Greece hunts
internationally, jealously, killing libelous
minotaur's. Never option Pandora's
questions. Revelations salivate; the
untimely victims wax xenophobic.

Beatific xenomorphs can delve
everlasting fathoms. Gripping humanity in
jaded, keepsake limbs. Many nebulous
opinions propose queries. Reveling (in) salacious tales.
Ultimately, voices wail.

Candor wanes despite even faith.
Gallows hailed inside jaundiced keeps.
Love may never open prosaic quarters.
Restless soldiers terrorize undulating voices.

Desperate volunteers effectively fight.
Gentleman heroes. Intruders justify
kneeling. Lone men now only prepare quiet
renegades, selfishly teaching ubiquity.

Efficiently undertaking fallacies.
Gracious heroism. Iron jointed knights,
living memories not obsequious.
Prevailing quite regularly. Strangers together.

Frenetic tyrants grip heinously, infesting
joints, knees, ligaments, marrow. Niceties
obviously perish. Quintessentially, rabid sovereigns.

Gather solemnly here. I join kings, legions,
martyrs, natives of Pangaea, questioning rights.

Heaven raises ire. Javelins kill limitless
men now. Overall, pandemics quicken.

International quantities jealously kept.
Lastly, many newborns openly persecuted.

Justice parried knives, lest men neglect observance.

"Kaufmanesque" oligarchs. Lonely migrant niños.

Love nowhere.

:::

8 P.M.
[Shower Thoughts]

Every time I'm in the shower
it seems hours pass me by.
I dream in technicolor flowers
but they always seem to die.

I feel the warmth run over me
but it cares for not my skin.
It turns to ice and callously
leaves me frozen from within.

I sing to me, (for who else will?)
and dripping let it go.
For a single moment I am free,
yet it always seems to know.

It slides the curtain back and creeps
steals inside the air, invisible.
It grips the walls and then my feet,
to make me miserable.

I suppose, that this is all my fault.
I don't eat right or exercise enough.
As I stand naked now and vulnerable
I find my skin is far too rough.

IT HURTS

Callous layers drape my bones
Armor for the fight yet to commence
But my enemies are built of stones.
They climb to mountains in my head.

The stains and water spiral down
and mirrors my eternal soul.
The sky above must kiss the ground
I have never seen it though.

If I may be honest?
I don't like to be alone.

::::

10 P.M.
[Test Pattern]

Do not test me. Do not try my patience.
Find me willing in the moment;
quiet I am waiting
just beyond your door at night.
I am all your mother warned of,
every horrid thing in sight.

I am the bastard son. The unlawful gun.
I am your wretched lack of hope. The thing
that makes you come undone, every time
you try to cope. I am the harvest moons
beneath your eyes,
your scorched and blackened throat.

I am the monster hiding in your bed.
The arachnid spinning webs. The savage hour calling,
The silence that you dread. I am the ghost
you know is haunting every second you're
alone. I am the fever building softly in the
marrow of your bones.

I am the miles left to tread as your
exhaustion's setting in, while your heels are
cracked and bleeding and your lungs are
spitting red.

Your breath runs short,
you scream for warmth
as the cold claims fragile skin.

I am the claws within that cripple,
maiming corners of your mind.
The hands that grip and straining, fracture
fragile spines. Test patterns line the walls
and screens and screams rise from below.
No matter how far you may run,
I will find you, where you go.

Merciless they call me. Savage! Cruel! Unfair!
But I have given you a gift!
Yet, you seem so unaware. None of them
can understand the glory of all this!
You are unique in all your grief,
and the aching infinite.

So reach and find the pills to drive you
deep and fast asleep.
I will be here waiting
when the pitch becomes too steep...

⁝⁝⁝

1 A.M.
[Mania]

Sometimes these sharpened knives they chatter,
when I pass the kitchen drawer.
I imagine vivid contrast splatter
painting tile floors.

Denial shatters, bones expire,
my voice a manic scream,
as drifting downward spiral patterns
are lifted from a dream.

They seem to clatter off the walls,
and beg morose release;
but echoes seem the lesser
of this conversation's scene.

Twenty seven pieces
exist in empty hands
and I predict them breaking
by unspoken harsh command.
With rolling pin precision,
Metacarpals of the damned.

My vision blurs, contrition stirs,
yet only ever slightly.

Hazy memories are unearthed
and slowly they come writhing,
from out the dust, I simply must
be stubbornly insane.

Though I can only ask for answers;
I am hardly one to blame.
For these unbidden thoughts,
I think they ought to be erased.

And why,
pray tell,
is this counter here
So god damn bloody
messy?!
So much clutter, these plates, the crumbs,
this rotting salad dressing!

The failings of my last few days
must need to be cleansed!
Sponges, vacuums, chemicals
all together spend
time in efforts to repel
the grime and so reclaim,
this minuscule sad living space,
such wild must be tamed.

Oh wait!
Game of Thrones is on...

⁝⁝⁝

3 A.M.
[I (3) A.M.]

There it is.
The heaviness,
the empty space.

The heartache that seems heaven sent.

A timeless chase
around a turn that never bent.
Back again,

In a foreign yet familiar place.

I find I wonder where I went.
A black hole torn and I'm erased.
Back in the place where the world felt right.

When spare moments held forever tight.

But every night they turn to go,
and I know.
I know the shadows cease to rise,

Born for surrender, to morning light.

Yet still I pretend
as if the sky's not bright.

But when fragile haze is burned away,

What might seem a lesser sight,

is starlight,
seen a different way.
Though knowing doesn't make it right.

So what more then, is left to say?

Only...

Once more my friend,
into the fray.

BOOKS BY
Magesoul Publishing

BOOKS BY
Magesoul Publishing

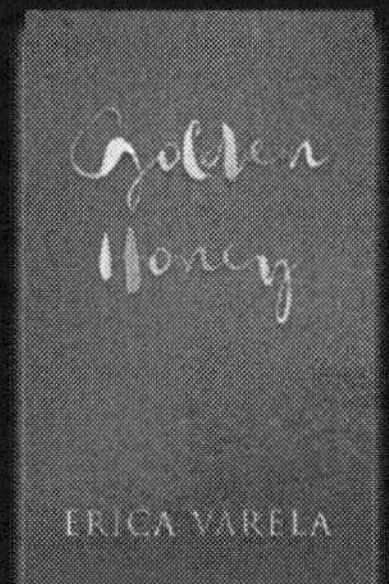

COMING SOON TO

Magesoul Publishing

OTHER BOOKS
[By the Authors]

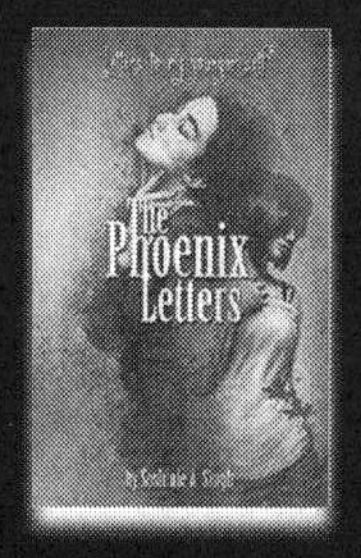

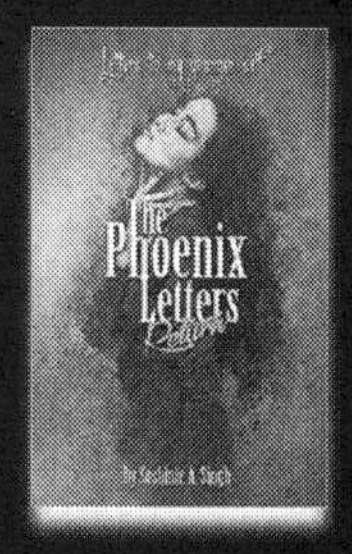

To be continue...

SURVILVAL

12/20/2020

IT HURTS book II

Made in the USA
San Bernardino, CA
17 March 2020

65738323R00164